Jenni James

MW00943011

The Bluestocking and the Dastardly, Intolerable Scoundrel

by Jenni James

This book is dedicated to Bailey McKayle, my own beautiful redheaded bluestocking.

And to Lacey Lamb, who without this perfect name, the book would not have been the same.

Acknowledgements:

To my most favorite Regency author, Judith A. Lansdowne. Without her delightful books, I never would have found my voice in clean literature. I love you. Thank you for your kindness and friendship.

Jenni James

Dear Reader,

   As I embarked on this new and adventurous journey of writing Regency romance, I wanted to create a series that would showcase my love of England and the joys I've felt while imagining her during the Regency period. For this very first book, I've gone out on a limb and chosen a real woman in history, though her name has been changed. She was an heiress, which was rare at the time, and a hidden bluestocking as well. It fascinated me to have a woman be so independent. Hence, the wonderful Lady Lacey Lamb was born, and what I envision her own romance must have been like. I hope you enjoy this new endeavor of mine and escape into a world that leaves you a bit happier and more hopeful than when you started the book.

   Love,

   Jenni James

Jenni James

CHAPTER ONE:

Lady Lacey Lamb, Viscountess Melbourne, was in high fidgets as she paced indignantly across the intricately woven rug in the library of her newly purchased townhome on Green Street. "Are you certain it was my name the insufferable swines were bandying about?"

She swirled around to face her second gardener, a respectable Mr. Toppens, who had only this moment returned from the errand she had sent him on earlier that morning. The old garden was in shambles, and one could not think when one's garden was in shambles, which is why it was imperative she bring up all of the gardening staff to the new home immediately. Toppens had been to fetch the seedlings she arranged to be picked up and had come back not only with the seedlings, but also with the most hideous piece of shameful gossip that had crossed this threshold yet.

"Yes, my lady. I came directly home soon as I heard." He fidgeted with his hat and stepped from one foot to the other.

"Thunderation!" she grumbled as she spun on her heel again, her brown muslin gown spinning with her. "Abominable. Unspeakable toads."

"Now, calm down," Pantersby, her normally sympathetic butler, attempted to soothe her. "You do not know the whole of it yet. It could be mere gabblemongers having a laugh at your expense."

"My expense! That is what causes me the most ire. No matter how anyone chooses to look at this, it has been done at my expense."

Both men jumped as she flung the small book she had been clutching upon the chiseled table before her.

This would not do. She was not some horrific shrew of a woman who shouted the place down. Placing her hand to her throat, she took a deep breath to calm the roaring of anger in her ears and struggled to ask coolly, her voice shaking a bit unevenly, "Tell me again, Toppens. What precisely did occur outside of White's?"

Toppens glanced anxiously at Pantersby and cleared his throat. "Lord Alistair Compton was in the midst of the throng."

"Are you confident it was him?"

"Yes, my lady. It was his height, standing a good head and shoulders above the rest—could not have been anyone else but he."

She nodded and closed her eyes. "Continue."

"He and a right large group of nobs came out of White's all boisterous and lively like, the whole lot of them laughing up a storm—never heard so much racket in my life. So, as I was waiting for the line of coaches to ease up a bit—seems as though everyone is coming to town today—I looked over and saw them all. And they were loud as crows, they were, shouting to the skies how as their betting at White's would give Lord Compton ten-to-one odds to get you, Lady Icey Lamb, Viscountess Melbourne, to fall dreadfully in love him by the end of the Season."

Apprehension gripped her chest as Lacey took another deep breath. This could not be happening. This simply could not be. "Icey? They think I am made of ice? Merely since I refuse to become a flirtatious chit in their presence? Now, because I declined to stand up with that buffoon Compton at Lady Huffington's ball, they must place wagers as if I were some token to be won? Infuriating villains. How dare they?" Lacey would have found another book to throw, but stopped herself. There was no need to ruin a perfectly magnificent library because of a bunch of nodcocks.

"'Tis why I came straight to you, my lady. I supposed you must know immediately to put this to stops."

"Yes." Her eyes lit up on the older silver-haired man. "Pantersby, is there anything that can be done?"

"Apart from castrating the lot of them?"

Lacey gasped and threw her hand to her mouth to stop the surprised giggle that was attempting this very moment to show itself. "Pantersby! Why, I never!"

He stood prim and proper, his uniform sharp, though one mischievous side of his mouth turned up the merest bit. "Yes, my lady?"

She gave in and a smile broke out, then a chuckle. Pantersby always had a way of helping her find the lighter side of any situation. But this was a larger mess than she had ever been in. Nonplussed, she sat down upon the nearest chair, her brown skirts in a wild array, as she took in the gravity of the situation. "Why can I not have peace?" She sighed. "This is precisely why I cannot abide *le beau monde* or the Season. I loathe coming here. A bunch of false gossipy twits trying to outdo each other in the most repulsive display of the marriage mart. Little gels with their hopeful mamas, wistful to catch the lucky looks of a mere stranger." She let out a very unladylike groan. "It is the most pitiful excuse of an existence there is—and I must endure it year after year."

"Well, if I may be so bold?"

She waved her hand. "Go ahead, Pantersby. You are most welcome to say whatsoever comes to mind, for nothing can be as dreadful as this. And Toppens, you may go. I thank you for the information. Though shocking, I am more grateful to have it than not."

Once the second gardener left, Pantersby continued, "You have two options here." He took a step forward. "You can pack up and run to the country again, as you are usually wont to do—this will force Lord Compton to forfeit his outrageous bet."

"Or?"

"You gird up your armor and stay to commence a battle."

Intrigued, Lacey sat up. "How so?"

"You teach that youth a thing or two about manners, for one. A bluestocking does not become a prestigious bluestocking because she is a simpleton. No, my lady, you have an opportunity to school the brat and set him down a peg or two."

One slim finger thoughtfully tapped her mouth. "I do have the upper hand, thanks to Toppens."

"That you do."

She scrunched her brow. "But I despise petty games like this."

"You can learn to enjoy them, you know."

"I can?" She stood up. There was no reason she should be in sulks over this. "So I can. And I will." She walked over to Pantersby and nodded once before stepping past him into the gallery. "I shall teach this dastardly, intolerable scoundrel the foolishness of placing one's bet before his comrades." A small grin began to form itself upon her features once more as an indignant brow arched. "Society may come and go as they please and attend their silly soirees and galas. I am here for Parliament alone. Women cannot yet attend, but the newspapers are quick in London, and my brother, Lord Melbourne, will continue to tell me the Whig ondits. I will have all the fascinating knowledge I need to entertain myself. However, this need not mean that I should be put out between sessions."

She walked to the center of the vestibule, placed her simple, unadorned bonnet atop her fiery red hair, and tied the bow rakishly to the side. Then she allowed Pantersby to slide her green woolen pelisse about her shoulders. "Please have Jameson bring the curricle around."

"Are you to go out alone, my lady?"

Lacey sighed as she tugged on her kid-leather gloves. "Do you think I ought not?"

"You know very well what I think. 'Tis too dangerous for you to be out and about without Mrs. Crabtree, or a footman at the least."

"If *men* can banter my name willy-nilly all over the place, I see no reason why it is not permissible to grant me the opportunity to defend myself and do the equivalent."

"You are not going to White's! 'Tis a gentleman's club. Please say that you are not."

Lacey closed her eyes and took yet another deep breath. Life was not just, and Pantersby was fortunate that she esteemed him as family or that outburst would have harmed him greatly.

"Begging your pardon, ma'am. I do not know what came over me."

She took her reticule from the same side table where all the rest of the folderols had been and then met his eyes.

"Do not worry. You are only attempting to make me see reason. To remind me of these confounded rules of town. No, I had not one notion to attend White's and place my own wager, making a fool and mockery of Lord Compton. Why should I ever do that?" Lacey tugged forcefully on her pelisse and gestured for Pantersby to open the door for her.

"No, I will allow my brother to avenge my wrongs. And as surely as I speak the truth of the matter to him, he will most certainly place the bet for me, and then Lord Compton and I will be on even ground, no?"

Pantersby gave a smug grin. "No, Lady Lamb. Not one whit of you shall be on even ground with such a man. Indeed, you are, and always will be, scores above him."

"Thank you, Pantersby."

He opened the door to the drudgery of London's finest attempts at weather and sent a footman scurrying to the lady's side to await the curricle.

"And what of the wager? Have you thought of a sufficient reply to his?"

Lacey smiled at the bottom of the steps of her new townhome and said, "Why, it will be to guarantee that he shall tumble topsy-turvy and head over heels in love with the Icey Lady Lamb." She chuckled at Pantersby's face above her. "The best part is, Pantersby, I have enough to my name that I can easily lose the despicable wager. Lord Compton, I believe, is such a wastrel of man, he does not. Either way, he fails, and perhaps next Season, he will learn to be a bit less of a libertine and more of a gentleman. Why, his mama may thank me when this is all through."

CHAPTER TWO:

Lord Alistair Compton, second son to the Marquess of Northampton, knew the moment he stood at the entrance of the Percevals' ballroom there was trouble afoot. Nearly eighty pairs of eyes fell upon him as the room tittered to a disconcerting stop. *Whatever could be amiss now?* He had definitely caught himself up most unwittingly in another grist for the mill. Pausing at the threshold of the grand ballroom, he gave a saucy grin and bowed low, showing off a handsome full head of raven-colored hair.

Instantly, fans began to flutter, and the orchestra started a quadrille. Though the dancers began to disperse once more and lead each other out upon the gleaming wooden floor, many gazes stayed fastened upon him.

Lady Perceval came to his rescue first, bustling up the side of the ballroom and past several whispermongers to greet him. "Why, Lord Compton, thank you for attending my sad little crush!" She chortled gaily up at him, her flushed, plump cheeks matching her rose-colored gown to perfection.

"I am most happy to be invited." He bowed over her hand and then asked, "Where is your husband? I do not see Henry anywhere amongst the throng."

She whipped open a fan and then hissed behind it. "He is trying to make up the damage done to you, sir."

Ah, just as he supposed. This was all to do about him. "And what damage is this?"

"Alistair!" She gasped, her fan quivering. "You do not know? Oh, good heavens. It is all that anyone is speaking of this moment." Pasting a smile on her face, she tugged upon his arm and nearly hauled him out of the room back into the hall where he had just been. Her eyes searched frantically up and down the large gallery. "Where is my wretched husband? He is never around when one needs him most."

"Shh…" he chided her. "There is enough gossip going at the moment—no need to sully your names as well. Henry is most likely hiding away in his study. I will go up and see if I can find him and ask what all this business is about, shall I?"

"His study? Yes. Yes, you are most likely correct. Go to him immediately." She shooed him with her hands. "I mean to obtain some semblance of normalcy down here, though I doubt I will be able to above half."

Georgianna Perceval was ever good at producing Cheltenham tragedies at the drop of a hat. This was probably nothing worse than a common misconception blown into ridiculous proportions. Compton chuckled as he made the steps two at a time up to the curmudgeon's hiding spot. He knocked twice before gently pushing the door open. "What is the meaning of this? I came to find one rapscallion and discovered three instead," he said as he looked between the lot of his companions sitting around Henry's table. "What great travesty could have happened to have you all here at once, instead of below dancing with the ladies?" Perhaps it was a bit more grave than he imagined.

"You," Lord Atten grumbled as he stood up and held out his chair for Compton. "Come and have a seat, old man. You will most definitely need it."

"Old? Twenty-six is merely one year older than you," he retorted as he sat into the high-backed chair. He glanced between Lord Hamson and Lord Perceval, both not quite meeting his eyes. "Whatever it is, it cannot be as appalling as your frowns. Now out with it. Which one of you will tell me why the world is staring at me as if I were an ape with two heads?"

Hamson rubbed his jaw. "In all the years I have seen stakes placed at White's, I have never come across something like this."

"Nor I," said Perceval.

"What is it? Are you attempting to drive me mad? What could be so scandalous as to leave you all utterly shaken?" Compton leaned back in his chair, taking on an air of nonchalance to cover the anxiousness growing within him.

Atten smirked. "It is best to say it than to piddle about as we are. Alistair, Lady Icey Lamb has placed her own atrocious wager in response to yours."

"Devil it!" Compton leaned forward. "I cannot imagine that even she would be so brazen."

"It was not her exactly," grumped Perceval as he shifted in his seat. "Nay, she had her brother Melbourne do it for her. Many are implying that she went to White's herself, but could not gain entrance, so she got her brother to do her dirty deed."

"And how did she find out?" Compton looked at all three, his countenance taking on a little smile. "I have to say, I am a bit chuffed. I would not have thought she had the pluck to do such a thing."

"You are laughing? Do you see this? Did I not say the same? Compton would laugh once we told him." Hamson smirked. "Well, you laugh now, for your head will be deep in the briars soon enough."

Compton let out a small snort, attempting to cover the chuckle lurking beneath. "Come now! Behold these scowls! How can none of you find this the least bit humorous? You have all become dead bores. Can you not comprehend the larks we can have with such a one as Lady Ice?" He stood up and did laugh heartily. "I can see from your expressions. I take it she has counter-wagered, no doubt saying it will be I who tumbles in love at her feet, no?" He could not keep his chortles down. This was too much.

"You are chirping merry. Look at you!" Hamson gasped as he attempted not to smile.

"No, I assure you, I have had nothing, not so much as a stitch of sherry today." He could not halt these absurd laughs. "I must say, I approve her aplomb, the preposterous chit. How remarkable that she would throw such a tosser." He gave a boyish grin as he sat back down in the chair. "Now tell me. What plans have we to thwart the enterprising minx? For you know, there is not one thing that satisfies me more than a challenge with a worthy opponent."

Perceval rested his elbows on the table. At nearly thirty, and most favorably married, he was the patriarch of their profligate group. "I cannot fathom why you do not cut your losses now and remove your bet from White's. 'Tis the gentlemanly thing to do. Quell the rumors and step down."

"Give up? Retreat? This is what you are asking of me? Nay. It would be deucedly bad form to pull out now."

Compton grinned. "It may be rather gauche of me, but I believe this Season shall turn out to be much more stimulating than I thought. Let the baggage attempt to entice me, for I am optimistic that my years of wooing the opposite sex are much more advanced than the icy infant could ever grasp. She will be in my arms before she knows what's what."

Atten pushed against Compton's chair. "Do you still mean to initiate your court with her tomorrow?"

"Of course. Johnson has the waistcoat chosen, and I plan to purchase a small posy for her as well, show up on her doorstop at two in the afternoon like a lovesick sop, and begin this joyous conquest." Compton stood up again. "No, gentlemen, nothing has altered. In fact, it has become even more apparent that I should move forward as planned. Not anything will stop me from facing this folly. It will be exceptionally grand; I can feel it now."

Hamson stood, clasped Atten's shoulder, and looked over to Perceval. "Never us mind this, for the more we attempt to make him see reason, the more the halfwit will hang himself."

"It is true," Atten said. "I am nearly tempted to go to White's myself and place my bet with the viscountess."

"Devil it!" Compton sputtered out a chuckle. "You scapegraces had better not leave me hanging, then."

"Leave you hanging?" Perceval got up and rounded the side of his desk. "We will stand there and watch as the Lady Ice draws and quarters you!"

CHAPTER THREE:

Only moments after Lacey had finished her tea with Mrs. Crabtree and was about to depart her home with two footmen to collect furniture for the new study she was putting in the master quarters, someone knocked upon the front door. She groaned at the top of the stairs and waited to hear Pantersby answer it.

Now that she had the notion to create one, she was very impatient to have her own study. There was no need for a second dressing room—a beautiful desk, shelves, comfortable chairs, and the like were precisely the thing. Her mother had passed away two years before, leaving her entailed to one of the few fortunes that were handed down through the women in her line, one that missed her half-brother Lord Melbourne completely.

With her new prestigious title also came a substantial pocket of wealth that she had been seeking to invest in various charities. However, her first major purchase was a house that was all hers. There were the two estates that came with the title, of course, but those were sprawling manor homes in the country. And while it is nice to reside away from the filth of London, there was also an excitement and buzz that is created in town that cannot be found anywhere else.

So many new government bills to contemplate and lobby for, so many new opportunities for growth and change for England. This was her passion—this was what captivated her most, the ondits of the political world, and what greater way to learn of it than to be right in the middle of all the hubbub during sessions of Parliament in the middle of the Season?

However, first things first. She simply must have a study in her chambers wherein to pore over the newspapers and articles about all that was going on.

So lost in her own thoughts, she had almost forgotten a visitor had come until she heard Pantersby welcome the scoundrel himself, Lord Compton! Frustrated, Lacey stepped back into her chambers and waited until Pantersby came and announced the vexatious man.

"Lord Compton is awaiting you in the green drawing room, my lady. Do you wish to visit with him, or are you indisposed today?"

"Tell him I am not at home. For indeed, two minutes earlier and I would have already been gone."

"As you wish."

Then just as suddenly, she changed her mind. Perhaps it would be best to meet with him. "No. Wait, Pantersby. I find do wish to speak to him. I will be down in a moment."

"Shall I bring in tea?"

"Certainly not. I have only this minute finished mine, and I do not believe the man deserves such courtesy. Either way, it does not signify, as he will be leaving shortly."

"Very good, my lady."

As soon as the butler left, she raced to her wardrobe and pulled out the closest thing that was fit for a morning call. Of all the silly nonsense. Why she felt the need to change was beyond her, but in this instance, it felt direly needed. Lacey rang for her lady's maid and between the two of them, they made fast work of her appearance, softening her hair and helping Lacey slip into a bright yellow gown with little bows along the flounce. It had been a gift from her mother, something she rarely wore, but it enhanced her red hair very nicely.

Curiosity got the best of her as she entered the green drawing room and found Lord Compton staring up at a portrait of her family above the mantel. She had brought it down with her from the country to make this place feel more like home.

The two footmen she had planned to take with her moments before now waited patiently inside the wide-open door, as Mrs. Crabtree was indisposed. So unused to callers was she, Lacey had almost forgotten she was not allowed to be alone with Lord Compton until she noticed them discreetly standing there.

"Good day," she said as she sat down on the large gold-and-green striped sofa. "And what brings you to my home?"

Compton turned around and bestowed a beautiful smile, and then with a swish, exposed a small posy. "I have come to beg forgiveness, Lady Lamb, for obviously offending you at the Huffingtons' ball last Wednesday. I let things settle a bit, and now I have come to see how you get on." He handed the flowers to her with a short bow. "And may I say how charming this room looks since you have taken it. You have done wonders with the place already. I am very impressed."

Lacey was nauseated by his drivel the second he opened his mouth. She pasted a smile on her face and said calmly, "Please be seated and stop this gibberish."

He arched a fine brow and took a step back. With his height, it would seem he was still too close to her. "What gibberish? I am genuinely paying you a compliment, and you treat me as though I am here for another design altogether." He had the audacity to look aghast.

"Pshaw." She waved her hand to indicate once more he could sit. "You are no sooner here to pay me compliments than I am here to receive them. Now out with it."

He sat his long limbs across from her in a matching green high-backed chair, and she was delighted to see that he seemed a bit put off. "Perhaps, my dear, if you learned a touch of manners and did not scowl so, you would be esteemed as a rare beauty here in town."

"Of all the preposterous things to say." She nearly lost her countenance as she attempted to keep a straight face. "You have gumption, I will give you that." She spun the little flowers around in her hand and then set them upon the small side table near her elbow. "So this is how you plan to woo me, then?"

Compton chuckled and audaciously leaned back in his chair. His dark hair contrasted greatly with green and gold. "Of course not, Lady Lamb. I have absolutely no notion of how to go about wooing anyone of your superior ilk. No, my dear, I am here because of a certain exhilaration to see how it is you plan on courting me."

Drat. The savage was attempting to throw her overboard, but it would not do. "My, my." She grinned. "Well, it would seem someone has been to White's and become aware of my brother's bet. I hope it was not too distressing to find that you had been bested, my lord."

He folded his arms and grinned in return. "I was fortunate enough to hear all about it last night at the Percevals' ball. Such a delightful way to receive knowledge of a growing quibble—whispers behind fans. Which reminds me, 'tis such a shame you were not there. You really should consider attending more than two of these events a year."

"Do you perchance miss being set down?" She blinked. "I could certainly do it again, if you wish."

Lord Compton leaned forward with an obnoxious, self-satisfied smirk upon his features. "That is the beauty of it, my dear. I no longer have to experience you cutting me when I request to take a turn about the dance floor. You have guaranteed that I will be granted as many fine dances with you as I choose."

Lady Lamb threw her head back, very unladylike, and laughed, truly laughed for the first time in days. The wily fox was indeed humorous, she would give him that, but he was definitely not worthy to be considered a significant challenge. "First, let me remind you that I am not your dear, so kindly stop referring to me as such. And secondly, Lord Compton, while I find your smugness entertaining, I do not for one moment believe your notions to be anything above that of a small child wishing for his own way. So if you will excuse me, I have other things to attend to today."

"How else are you to win my heart if you do not show me some affection?" the disagreeable man countered, as if she had not said another word.

She shook her head slightly and smiled her dazzling smile—the one that transformed her into her mother, a diamond of the first water in her day. "You, silly couth, seem to have failed to recognize the irony here. I do not have to win your heart. You only have to fall at my feet and beg me to join you in matrimony." Lacey allowed her own smug smirk to show upon her face. "And as far as the *ton* is concerned, you are already doing so by scraping about for attention at my door. For why else would you be here?"

Jenni James

CHAPTER FOUR:

Instead of Compton taking his leave, as polite manners would suggest he do, especially as the lady herself was wont to be elsewhere, Lord Compton eased himself more fully into the chair and stared at his opponent. Despite having unfashionably ginger-colored hair, Lady Lamb was exceptionally striking to look upon. Indeed, notwithstanding her icy nature, they would have been better to have named her Lady Fire than Lady Ice. Not for one moment did he believe himself to be bested by her. She was as amusing as he had hoped she would be, and for that he was grateful, but to assume she believed herself to be at a greater advantage than he—nonsense. Lady Ice was ever as inconsequential as he first knew her to be.

It was time, however, to put a bit of a hiccough in her designs. "Come with me for a drive around Hyde Park this afternoon."

"Certainly not." Lady Ice raised her chin a notch.

Compton was not to be deterred. "Why ever not? Are you running crow?"

"I am not troubled by you, or whatever appalling thing you plan to include me in. I never have gone around Hyde Park in a curricle during the fashionable hour. I detest such flamboyant, pompous traditions, and I always will. If I am to visit a park, I would much rather walk in clothing that can weather the terrain and explore the place, not be seated beside a sniveling man as I wave politely to everyone else making a similar spectacle of themselves. It is quite beyond me why anyone would care for such a thing. To be seen? Goodness, why should one care if one is seen? In my opinion, it is the epitome of gossipy fluff."

Intrigued, he asked, "How so?"

"Why, you are simply asking others to blather on about you. A person goes to Hyde Park to be talked about. I, however, would prefer to enjoy myself."

"I have never heard a woman speak as you do."

She chuckled and brushed at an imaginary speck of dust on her yellow skirts. "What? Blatantly calling out the abysmal practices of society?"

"No, with sense."

That seemed to perk her up a bit, for she tilted her head and cautiously asked, "What do you mean?"

He laughed. "No man in his right mind enjoys parading about Hyde Park. We all wish to be elsewhere, but we do it to keep our mamas happy and to pay court to the ladies." He adjusted in his seat to turn more fully toward her. "Yet, now to find a lady who finds it as tedious as we do—it is by far the most intriguing thing you have said."

"I have many intriguing things to speak of, I am sure. But you, sadly, will never hear them. I prefer to be alone and to go about my world with independence, thank you."

"But are you ever lonely? You cannot be as old as me, yet surely you are not far off from my twenty-six. Have you never considered marrying someone and settling down?"

[23]

"Are you coming to scratch so soon, my lord? I honestly feared it would take much longer. La! But this is so much nicer. The answer is no. You may inform everyone that I have officially won the bet."

"You know very well that I was not offering for your hand, you monstrous brat."

She gave him a sharp look. "No, you were daring to insult me by assuming someone at my age must be eager to plunge into marital bliss," she countered. "Which led me to turn the tables and remind you to behave."

"Nothing of what we have spoken of signifies that either of us will conduct ourselves politely. If anything, it merely sets us up to continue to spew more drivel at the other."

"I do not speak drivel, my lord. I am in earnest when I relay that I have no desire to go for a ride around Hyde Park. I have explained my wishes to you, and my reasons for doing so. I assumed we had finally found some common ground when you deemed it necessary to imply that I was growing too ancient and must hurry and marry or there would be no hope for me. Has it ever occurred to you," she continued, "that I have no desire of any kind to wed?"

"But why? Honestly, I do not imply anything insulting—I am genuinely confused. Why would a handsome woman, with wealth and privilege and a title, not wish to marry and make a name for herself? Now, halt. I can see I have somehow offended you once more, and that is certainly not my intention. Let me finish. I am mostly curious as to why you have not wed when one of your character and intelligence could influence a husband, and therefore help transform England into a better nation."

Lady Lamb clutched her fists upon her lap. "Are you saying I should marry a member of the House of Lords or the House of Commons? Why would *you* care about England's improvement? As far as I can see, you are nothing but a wastrel of a man who spends more time making notorious bets at his club, losing money he can ill afford, than caring about the political issues of this country!"

Abruptly, he stood up. It was too much. Her opinions and scant beliefs of him were much too hard to hear from her lips. "Forgive me, Lady Lamb. I have trespassed on your hospitality far too long. Thank you for your patience. No need to call for your butler—I shall see myself out." Compton's chest tightened uncomfortably and his stomach twisted as he bowed over the lady's hand. He had one thought, and it was simply to escape these confoundingly claustrophobic walls.

If he learned anything in those wasted, tedious minutes, it was to understand precisely why she had not been courted, and why she still remained unwed. For what man could ever put up with such boorish opinions and harsh realities as she provided? For a minute there, he felt he was sitting across from his father!

"Lord Compton," she called as he headed toward the door of the drawing room. He paused, almost willing to ignore her, and then turned slightly. "Yes?"

Lady Lamb was up and walking toward him, her hand out. "Will you please shake hands with me?"

His gaze met with the bluest of eyes he had ever beheld. For a moment, they were genuinely breathtaking. How had he never noticed her eyes before? Instinctively, his hand came out to clutch hers.

"I did not mean to insult you." A wary smile lifted the corner of her mouth, but it was the drawn-in brows of concern that fascinated him. "I know I am brusque at times." Her voice was soft and gentle. "But please understand, I thought I was within the rules of the game. We were both slinging spirited mud at the other, you see? I beg your pardon if at any moment, my words harmed you."

For a few piercing seconds, stabs of guilt barraged Compton as he stood there holding her delicate hand in his. Here was the woman he had publically shamed and mocked, begging his forgiveness for privately holding her own and sending him running. There was no need for her apologies, or for her to feel wrong for her comments. He was everything she had said and more, everything he despised most about himself, and everything no other peer would have had the gumption to express.

He brought that gloveless hand up to his lips and kissed the back of it. "There is nothing to express regret over." Then he attempted a smile, yet his heart was much too ashamed to make decent work of it, he was sure. "Although you have successfully gained a point in your favor, you have not won yet. I shall return."

And then he was gone. Across her threshold and hastily making his way down the street to cool his ever-whirling head. He needed space. He needed to breathe. He would come by later for his curricle. For now, he must chase these demons away before they caught him up and made him answer for all the misgivings he was feeling.

CHAPTER FIVE:

Compton walked blindly until he made it to the back end of Hyde Park where Green Street connected. There he took Lady Lamb's advice to explore and came off the path into the brush and trees and found a large boulder to sit upon, away from the noise, and muddle over his fate.

He was not one to reflect deeply on the past, nor was he one to believe his mistakes were worthy of contemplation and reform. However, it was the way she said it—as if it were purely matter-of-fact—that plunged right through him. Had he truly become what his father was worried about most? A gambling, mad wastrel? The old Marquees had always wanted him to go into the House of Lords—it was his dream for him. And how Compton had loved that dream. He even went to school for it. Yet, Compton could not find much use for it now. It was one thing to upset Lady Ice with talk of marrying men who could change the world. It was quite another to be given goose for the gander and have the conversation flipped back onto him.

He sighed and rubbed his hand over his face. Not even twenty minutes in the lady's home, and he was already feeling a dashed mite more stupid than he had that morning.

As he was contemplating this particular notion of foolishness, Compton heard strange whimpering noises not far from where he was sitting. In the space of a minute, he came to himself enough to realize they were cries of distress. Crouching down on a section of dirt, no doubt ruining his buff pantaloons, he lifted up a branch and found a whole litter of newly born puppies. The little tykes, with their eyes still closed, could not have been more than a week old. But where was their mama? Surely she would have growled her warning at him as soon as he attempted to sit down so near the little family.

Glancing around, he could not make out hide nor hair of where she could be. He debated Johnson's shock if he arrived home with the infant litter. *No doubt he would attempt to have my guts for garters for ruining my nice new coat.* But it simply could not be helped. He could not abandon the destitute pups. After a few more frantic moments of searching, he found their mama too, concealed below the opposite side of the same bush far beneath the thick fronds. She was clearly emaciated and unwell. Her breathing was labored, and she could not move her head much to look at him. Those puppies of hers must have taken the last bit of life she had from her. Poor dears.

"Well, you'd best come home with me, then, though I am certain to hear about this for a long while."

Compton took off his new coat and gently gathered up the fragile dog in his arms, and then fished around until he found each of the five multi-colored puppies under the shrubbery, plopping them upon their mama. Then he wrapped the lot snugly up and carried it back the two hundred yards or so to Lady Lamb's house to fetch his curricle.

There was not a stable boy to be seen, so he made his way up the steps and rapped with the brass door knocker.

When the butler opened the door, the man was clearly flummoxed to find Lord Compton in just his shirtsleeves, his arms laden, but Compton could not worry overly much about that. "I left my curricle in the yard. Could you be so kind as to have it brought round?" he said as his bundle began to whimper and move precariously under the wool of his coat.

"Best step inside. Lady Lamb will be anxious to see you."

"Not to be contrary, but perhaps not in my present attire. I do not wish to astonish the lady." Compton grinned and then dipped quickly to catch an escaping scoundrel before he tumbled out.

The butler's eyebrows rose. "Indeed, Lady Lamb is rarely astounded by anything. Whatever you have in there will most likely fall to its death if you do not come in and set it down. Come." He opened the door wide, and Compton followed him back into the drawing room where he had been not thirty minutes before.

"Are you certain you want me here in all my dirt?"

"Lady Lamb would have my head if I sent you anywhere else. The drawing room will do."

As soon as the man left, Compton knelt upon the floral rug and began to unwrap his parcel with the hopes of righting the lot of them.

"What is this?" asked Lady Lamb as she came into the drawing room dressed in a much plainer brown gown than what she had worn earlier.

"Confounded puppies. Forgive my attire." Compton would have stood to receive her, but just then, one of the little monsters scooted off his mother and rolled to his coat and then toppled onto the rug.

"Oh, my!" the lady giggled.

"Now, now, you remain where I put you," he said as he scooped the rascal up. "All of you must assist in keeping your mama warm. She is not well, and you are blind as bats and cannot even see what you are about."

"Goodness," Lady Lamb gasped as she knelt on the floor next to him. "She is starving. Why did you not say something immediately?" She turned toward the door. "Pantersby, see that a cloth and warm saucer of milk is brought here directly."

"Yes, my lady."

"However did you find them?" she asked him as she began to help collect the wiggly pups.

He ruefully grinned. "I left my curricle here and did as you proposed—I walked into Hyde Park and explored the area, and came across the imps whimpering incessantly."

"What a find. You truly did go exploring." She ran her hand over the mother and whispered sadly, "I fear she will not make it."

"Aye. I fear it too, which is why I must bring the lot of them home with me immediately, only stopping here to fetch the curricle." He glanced over at her. "And then I promise that I and my sad state of dress shall leave."

"Do they have to go? I would love them." Lady Lamb put her hand to her mouth. "Pardon me. I am being entirely too impulsive by half. I do not know what I would do with a full litter and their failing mama. Besides, you have found them first—they are yours to claim, and forgive my hastiness. I did not think before I spoke."

Pantersby approached with the milk.

"Thank you." She gave him a grateful smile and then surprised Compton when she asked her butler to stay and see if he could be of any assistance.

The older man flipped his coattails and then joined them upon her rug as if he had done so a thousand times. "This dog is in very dire straits indeed. She would not have lasted another night. It was good of you to rescue her." The man looked straight at Compton and gave a short, proud nod.

Compton, who had never had such a familiar moment with any of his staff, found it oddly comforting. "Thank you. I am very worried for her."

Lady Lamb lifted the mama's head gently and slid the saucer under her nose. Eagerly, the dog lapped, but then just as suddenly stopped. Her breathing became more pronounced. "What should we do?" All thoughts of their previous disagreements flew from his head as he beheld the charming picture of the lovely Lady Ice holding the small canine and her butler attempting to wrangle the whining pups.

"These little ones are thirsty too. We will get Cook and her girls to see if they can help feed them," Pantersby observed as he petted them. He glanced over at their mama, who was even then endeavoring to lap up more milk. "Ah, there she goes. Good girl! If she continues to rally, as it looks like she will, she will come out of it and these scamps will grow to be great big naughty balls of fluff in no time."

"Do you think so?" Compton asked with a bit more hope than he dared to imagine.

"Yes, right as rain they will all be in the next couple of days. Mark my words—I have helped many a pup in my time. See how the mama continues to drink? It is good. She will get her strength back shortly, and then we will know trouble."

Compton picked up one of the babes and nestled it near his shoulder. "How so?"

"Why, the whole place will be overrun with adventurous mites attempting to tumble the house down."

"Oh, how fun that would be!" Lady Ice laughed, a genuinely enchanting laugh—one that made her blue eyes sparkle as she continued to hold the mama's head.

Then a very bizarre thing happened. Lord Compton's heart gave a teensy jump of warmth as the rascal in his arms began to nuzzle against his neck, and he found himself laughing with her.

CHAPTER SIX:

Lady Lamb observed the pompous Lord Compton and continued to giggle as he attempted to appear up to snuff in his shirtsleeves and puppy kisses, kneeling upon her floor. She had never thought he could look so completely human.

"Come on you, take a little more. You have almost got it," she coaxed the malnourished pooch who had nearly drunk the whole plate of milk. The mama's poor fur was matted and awfully muddy. In fact, Lacey was not certain what color the canine actually was. The little puppies were an assortment of browns, black, and white. Therefore, there was no telling what her coloring was. The poor dear thing must have been lying in the mire waiting for a passerby to find her for some time.

Lacey's gaze wandered back to Lord Compton and marveled for a moment at the heart of a man who would go out of his way to rescue such a rambunctious load. He may be a ne'er-do-well, but he undeniably had a heart under all those perverse inclinations. A heart that mayhap allow her to keep the sweethearts in her home? He had not answered her about the pups, and had not thought to

Jenni James

discourage Pantersby when he offered to help. Taking courage, she attempted again. "What will you do with them? Have you decided?"

Grinning, Lord Compton looked up from the puppy's affection and shook his head. "I cannot imagine what my valet will say to this, nor my butler, for that matter. They will undoubtedly have my head."

"They are so darling. Once they are nourished properly, I believe Mama here will take care of the lot of them, and you will have no trouble at all."

"Would you be so kind as to take them in?" Lord Compton asked. "I know we have our differences. However, Pantersby mentioned that your cook and girls might help."

"Oh, we would be delighted to! Yet I do not desire to take something so grand as this from you." Surely he must want them for himself.

He grimaced with a slight air of indifference. "I fear I am ill equipped to take care of them all, though if you are against it, my staff will get on reasonably well."

Her eyes met his dark ones, and she could see a spark of something lurking deep within. "Why, you are telling a whopper!"

"And what would make you imply that?"

"I do not know the reason you are doing such a thing, but you wish to keep these sweetlings as much as we do, and yet you are willing to give them up. Why?"

Lord Compton grinned handsomely at her and shrugged one shoulder. "Can I not propose a bit of a peace offering for the manner in which I left so suddenly earlier?"

Lacey could feel her face paling as she recalled the flippant statements she had made. Certainly she had been cross with him and thought to discompose him a bit.

However, her intention was never to truly wound the fellow.

Pantersby shifted and cleared his throat. "I shall run and get some more milk, and let Cook and her girls know we have visitors. They will be so pleased." Then he turned to Compton. "That is, if you are certain we are to keep them, my lord?"

Compton nodded. "No, it makes much more sense to leave them here than to attempt to bring them all home. The less they are shaken about, the better, I think."

Once her butler left, Lacey brought the subject back around, feeling the need to beg forgiveness. "Please do not speak of that now. I am overly ashamed at my reply to you."

Compton gave a short, forced laugh. "What did you say that I did not need to hear?"

"My lord, I . . . pardon me."

"No. You were correct. I am worth nothing, and after all these years, I have become even further from myself than I would have ever imagined."

Lacey's chest tightened at his response, and she looked down at the puppies, not sure how to reply. They had begun to tire out. Three of them had discovered a spot to nestle next to their mother and were slumbering peacefully, their little bellies moving up and down.

"Very well, rascal. I fear it is time for you to join your family as well," Lord Compton said as he added his sleeping mite to the pile. The puppies whimpered in protest for a moment as their brother joined them, and then one by one, quieted down and nuzzled back adorably into each other.

She watched them a minute or two, her heart marveling at the joy of such a sight, and then whispered,

"They appear so peaceful. I truly believe nothing cheers the soul more than being near baby animals."

She caught Lord Compton's eye before he took a deep breath and said, "The whole lot is a filthy muddle. I fear your carpet may never be the same if we do not transfer them somewhere else."

"Your coat is already most likely ruined."

"Yes, I know. Johnson will certainly ring a peal over my head for it too. He is always too stuffy when it comes to my clothing."

She grinned. "I cannot imagine anyone having words with you and endeavoring to put you in your place."

His eyes met hers with a mischievous gleam. "Unless it is you, of course."

"I do not count. I doubt there will ever be a time when I am not willing to give you a piece of my mind."

"True! And what would be the fun in that if you did not?"

She glanced away. He was attempting to be kind, and though sweetly meant, it was not needed. "I am certain you will have reservations about crossing my appalling path in the future."

"Correct. You have given me pause for thought. However, I was hoping I might be able to come and visit as the puppies are growing."

A warmth spread through her. She had given him every opportunity to drop this charade, and yet he did not. Mayhap his need to win was greater than his pride after all. Lacey pretended to contemplate it a moment before teasing him. "So was this your ploy all along? Did you hide this particular family in the park in hopes that you could use them to woo me?" She chuckled at his stunned face. He evidently thought—for a brief instant—that she was serious, but then he calmed a little.

"What? Do you not remember me announcing 'tis you who will be courting me?"

She laughed. "Ho! My lord, I do remember some brief nonsense of the sort. However—"

He rudely interrupted. "Who is to say that you did not place the mama and her puppies under that bush so I would find them and lose my heart to the lot of you? How can I be certain this was not *your* dubious plan all along?"

"You are a scapegrace!" she replied humorously.

Then she watched as Lord Compton's face took on a bit of seriousness as he asked, "Lady Lamb, would you like to tour Hyde Park with me tomorrow to see what other mischief we can find?"

She sat up, her heart beating a bit more forcefully. "Do you mean, exploring off the beaten path?"

"Precisely."

Cautiously, she asked, "And what will this gain for either of us?"

"Do we have something to lose by doing so?"

She blinked and stared at him and his logic. "I suppose not. It is merely a walk through Hyde Park."

"No, my lady, you are most certainly offered a traipse through the park. Walking is what all the other boring polite society will be achieving."

She worried her lip a moment and then asked, "Could we go a little earlier than planned, though? I would much rather it not be during the fashionable hour. And four is really way too late. The papers will be in then, and I—" She stopped. Not because she was ashamed, or uncomfortable, but only because she was not certain he would care to hear her reasons to be at home by four in the afternoon.

"Papers? The news, Lady Lamb?"

"Er, yes." She studied the dirty coat before her.

"You wish to be home to read the news? Not to wait until later in the evening, but precisely at four o'clock when the papers are delivered?"

"Four eighteen, four twenty around here."

He took on an air of astonishment. "Very well. If the lady cannot wait another moment to read the papers, who am I to keep her away from them?"

She flushed. "Do not mock me, my lord."

"I most certainly am not. I find you fascinating and interesting—there is no mocking. But I see that you come by the name of bluestocking rather well."

"Thank you." Whether or not he meant such a statement as a compliment, she would surely accept it as such, for there was no greater esteem than through one's wisdom. "I have always loved to learn. When school was completed, I wished more than anything I could continue on and go to Cambridge, or Trinity, or King's College, or even Oxford like you gentlemen."

"You are in earnest. You actually desired to have studied more?"

"Yes. It is enthralling to absorb so much."

He shook his head. She almost made him wish he had remained at his studies longer and become a scholar. Almost. He cleared his throat. "So will you come with me to Hyde Park tomorrow at noon?" Compton all but grimaced as he said it. He rarely woke before noon. However, perhaps it would not be difficult to give an exception this once.

CHAPTER SEVEN:

Lacey caught her breath at his repeated proposal of an outing to Hyde Park. She gently ran her hand over the slumbering canine and kept her focus there as she responded, "I thank you for asking me, for frankly you have gone out of your way to do so, and adapted to suit me, but I must decline."

"Are you otherwise engaged tomorrow?"

She could easily tell a small fib and say yes. Lacey looked into his dark eyes and then shook her head. "No. I do not—I would hope not—no."

"You are not quite ready to be in my company, then?"

"Yes. That is it precisely."

He ruefully grinned and touched two fingers to his brow a mock salute as he bowed his head. "As you wish."

There was a short, awkward pause before Pantersby returned with more milk, and then Lord Compton stood and bid his adieus.

"No need to remove my coat from beneath the mongrels just yet. I will come to collect it another day."

"But the curricle is open, sir!" Lacey replied. "Would you not do better to have some sort of covering? Or take one of my coaches instead."

"You are kind. Yet, with all the rumors the gossipmongers have wagging about, leaving your house in my shirtsleeves and dirt ought not add more to the fire than what is already there."

The *ton* and their need to be in everyone's business would forever vex her. "Let them think what they will, then. I have no need to be ashamed of your attire if you are not."

He bent low and kissed her hand. "I will pull the top of the thing up to give me some semblance of a roof, and hopefully hide the worst of my wear, anyhow. Farewell, Lady Lamb. Until our paths cross again."

Even though there was a slight hollowness in her chest at refusing him, she did not have any regrets. They could not become on too easy of terms, or this could grow confusing for them both. No, it was best that they keep a moderate distance. And with the puppies being here, it would seem they would be close enough as it was.

By the time the canines were bathed and cuddled into their new warm bed by the kitchen fire, it was way too late for Lacey to pick up the furniture she had been eagerly awaiting that morning. Which was probably for the best, since it was looking to be a long night nursing the adorable multi-colored babies and their cinnamon-and white-colored mother back to health.

At half past midnight, she began to make her way up to bed, first stopping into the library to check on the day's mail. Lacey was shocked to find several of the *ton's* invitations out into society upon the small silver plate on the table. "Pantersby," she called before she realized he was most likely preparing the house for the night.

"What is it, my lady?" he asked a bit breathlessly.

"Good heavens. Forgive me—I did not mean to make you run all the way here in this state to hear me whine about a few invitations."

"What is amiss?" he asked, not willing to admit to being disturbed.

She held up the plate. "I am at a loss as to explain why this server is so full."

"It would seem the elite desire to see you and Lord Compton make lovesick fools of each other." He grinned and cleared his throat. "In my opinion, I feel it is about time you are included in their inanity."

"But you know I despise these things." She pulled out four or five of the thick vellum requests. "It is preposterous to expect me to come."

"Then do not go, my lady. Simply cry off from them all and send your regrets."

"It is excessively tempting to do just that. You have no idea."

"I fear I do." He walked into the room and gathered a few of the ones she had not touched. "Though, perhaps you can pick and choose which hostess you are willing to give the pleasure of your company. There are at least three here I would be loath to reject on your behalf."

"And why is that?"

"Because these are the wives of the lords who sit in Parliament, and Lord Stanthorpe is the Speaker of the House, my lady."

"Oh!" Her eyes went wide. "And will their husbands be there as well?"

"Depending on what the request is for, but at any dinner or ball, you can be certain to see them."

Lacey took the offered invitations and swiftly opened them.

"I am not certain I have the wardrobe for this type of existence," she fretted.

"Then perhaps it is time to update it."

Lacey groaned. "Why is this world so demanding? Why can I not simply walk anywhere just as I am?"

One of Pantersby's large gray eyebrows rose with a look of disdain upon his features.

She laughed and tossed an invite toward his head.

He easily caught it and then placed it on the table. "Think about it. Do not answer back quite yet. And you might as well wait and see what tomorrow brings before you decide."

"Do you think there will be additional invites?" She could not fathom more. As it was, she had received more in one day than she would have in three years.

"Of course there will be others. You, my lady, have become the *ton's* most sought-after guest."

"I will become the *ton's* most sought-after fool. Thunderation! And I presume I will have to behave like a lady as well," she moaned. "How is one supposed to recollect so many rules of etiquette?"

* * *

Lord Compton's nightly routine did not fare as stimulating as Lady Lamb's. In point, after his valet, Johnson, had tut-tutted over the disgraceful state of his clothing, Compton slipped into a dressing gown and endeavored to be a bit more cordial to his butler when Terrell came to see that all was well for nightfall.

"Terrell, stop for a bit and speak with me." Compton gestured toward the matching chairs in his bedroom and sat down on one himself.

"My Lord?" Terrell asked. "Have I done something to offend you?"

"No, no. Come and sit. I merely meant to ask for some advice."

"Advice, my lord?"

"Yes. Take up a chair and converse with me."

"I would much prefer to stand. I cannot fathom sitting next to you, my lord."

"Come now. I insist! Am I as daunting as all that?"

"Not precisely, though I am uncertain as to why you are insisting. Are you confident I have done not a thing to trouble you?"

"No. It is about Lady Ice." He gave up attempting to have the butler sit. Apparently, some rules are hard to break between the gentry and the serving class. "I have offered to take her to Hyde Park the exact way she said she would love to go, and yet, she refused me."

Terrell fidgeted, but was obviously curious. "What do you mean, 'exact way'?"

"It would seem Lady Lamb does not prefer to be seen riding about in a curricle so that all of London may gossip about her." Compton stared at his butler, waiting for the man to say something.

He started and then cleared his throat. "Well, that seems like a right smart lady to me."

"To me as well. I even told her so. She then said she would much rather go traipsing through the park and not merely riding. How going off the beaten path would be much more diverting than scads of people offering pleasantries to each other."

Terrell looked at him expectantly, almost waiting to see if he could speak. Compton grinned. "Out with it, then."

"So you requested her to go explore the park with you as an alternative, and she still said no?"

"Precisely. Why do you think that was? She said she was not prepared to be seen with me yet, but I cannot gather if that is really the case."

"My lord, if you had been mocked and wagered against and then had your quiet life completely upheaved by the very person who was attempting to harm your reputation most, would you then wish to be near his company so much? Or even so intimately as to do something you found utterly enjoyable? Would you not rather spend pleasurable moments with those you truly respected and esteemed than with the enemy?"

Compton sat for a full minute and did merely blink as he took in the man's words.

Clearly fearing he had overstepped his bounds, Terrell bowed and said, "Forgive me. I will attend to my duties now, my lord, and I assure you to never speak about such things again."

Compton shook his head and glanced up. "No. I thank you for your honesty. Something may be hard to hear, but that does not mean it is not meant to be heard. Again, I thank you. You are a good man, Terrell. Nay, you are a respected friend, for you have expressed to me the truth."

CHAPTER EIGHT:

Pantersby proved to be correct. Lacey received several more invitations the following day, and then by time the week was over, the vellum missives nearly tripled. "For heaven's sake, do you think they will continue to plague me? How is one to attend so many events?" she asked Pantersby as she combed through them whilst perched on the large chair in the library.

"One does not," he answered haughtily as he approached with the afternoon tea.

Lacey smiled in relief. "Do I have to answer each one? Oh, then I can easily toss them all and be on my way."

"If you wish." He poured the tea and set it down with a saucer on the fine table near her elbow. "Though, perhaps it would not be the best notion to completely shun all of the hostesses. And do not overlook the fact that there are a few you will wish to attend."

"Oh, yes. I had forgotten about the political families. Please, will you place two sandwiches on my plate this time? I find I am quite famished after repositioning the furniture about in my new study, though I am not certain when I will be able to enjoy it. The wallpaper smells rather dreadful."

Pantersby placed the sandwiches on a pretty plate on the table and added a bowl of fruit and another with Cook's perfected sweet biscuits. "Do you need help deciding which invitations you should accept?"

"Is it wrong that I know the names of all the men, yet have never thought to learn their wives or their houses to identify an event they are hosting?" She flipped another missive upon the table.

"Well, it does prove to be a bit of a hindrance." Pantersby grinned beneath his frown.

"I see that smile you are attempting to hide. I know what you are thinking there."

"Oh, do you? And I was not attempting to hide anything. Merely feeling a bit pleased that this moment has come back around again."

"What do you mean?" she asked and then pointed to the chair. "No one is around. Sit down and chat with me for a little while."

He shook his head. "I have many duties to attend to still."

Apprehensively, she glanced up at him. "Are you overworked? Do you need respite? You are welcome to add more to the staff if you require."

"Separately from the three we have already employed the last two days? You and your requirement to hire every imp and urchin we come across."

She could not help herself. "Pantersby, you know very well I could not leave those two young lads to starve out on the street. They were penniless beggars. Their own father had deposited them in the center of London and told them to get on with life and to find work." Her stomach churned at the thought of the mere eight- and ten-year-old boys struggling to make sense of what had happened to them without a thing to their name except the garments on their backs.

Lacey set her teacup on the tabletop and slumped into the chair. "This is an additional cause for why I cannot abide London. One can hide in the country well enough and enjoy the simplicity of life and go about caring for your neighbors and the parish without ever truly knowing the cruelties that await here."

She shuddered and brought her arms in close. "How many children have been treated to the same? It cost me fiddlesticks to bring those boys into the home and set them to working in the stables."

"Aye." Pantersby nodded. "They now have beds, uniforms, prestige, and pocket money."

"They have food and a place that will always be a refuge for them." Lacey took a deep breath. "England must change her ways. There must be hope for the very deprived, or more and more children will be discarded in the heart of her and left for whoever wants them most." Panic started to swell in her chest. "I cannot take the thought, Pantersby. I cannot even fathom such a horror." The image of the boys' frightened looks as they shared their story with her flooded her memory. For two days, they assumed their father would return. By the third day, they had begun to wander. When she had seen their huddled forms against the stone fence and required her driver to stop, the boys were quite lost from wandering and terribly cold from the rain and damp earth they had been sleeping on.

Her heart could not comprehend such cruelties. "I knew I was loved," she blurted out passionately as her voice trembled. "It makes me want to go out on the street corners and guard them all."

"You are a good lady. A grand one with an enormous heart, and you will always be thought of amongst the servants as the most generous of all the nobility."

She shook her head. "It is not enough. It is not."

Pantersby finally sat down in the chair near hers and reached over and touched her arm. "Do you recall the lessons I taught you all those years ago?"

"Yes." She sniffled and blinked away her impulsive emotions. "You were the best of tutors. You did not stop like the others had. You continued to teach me more and more and more."

He chuckled and nodded slowly. "You were unlike any pupil I had ever had. Such an earnest need for knowledge. Do you ever marvel why I was so eager to answer your advertisement in the papers?"

"Because you had become mad?" She grinned to take the sting out of her reply. "Pantersby, I worry. I did not want to hire you as my butler, but—"

"I was insistent. I had retired and found little purpose in my life and was bored to tears until I read the papers and found you were looking for help. It was the solution—the natural transformation I was searching for."

"And now? Do you regret being my servant? You know my qualms and quibbles and all those irksome notions I have. Do you ever wish you could toss it all and leave and never glance back?"

"Every single day I have known you, similar thoughts have crossed my mind." He threw his head back and laughed. "No, Lady Lamb, I am teasing you. There have been only a few days when I have been frustrated, and those seem to be the days when I am reminded once again how kind your heart is and what a remarkable lady you have turned out to be, and all at once, I find I am your champion."

She picked at her plain brown muslin gown. "Occasionally, when I was young, I would envision you to be the father I was never acquainted with."

"Your father loved you. He did not understand you, and was often away, but he loved you still."

She sighed. "My father was more involved with politics than nurturing a family. 'Tis why I could never have children of my own."

"I would not say never." One eyebrow of his quirked. "Lord Compton displayed a very fine worth when he brought the puppies back with him."

"And whatever in the world do you mean by that?"

"I suppose we will have to see."

"Pantersby…"

"Yes?"

"You will not tell me, will you?"

"Tell you what?" His eyes twinkled as they were wont to do when she was little.

She would never win this squabble in a thousand years. "Oh, I give up. How are the puppies adjusting? I have not been down to see them since this morning. Is Mama still doing well?"

"Like a champ, she is. Got up on all fours earlier this afternoon. The cook's girls were squealing with excitement and nearly shouted the place down with their shrieks."

"Good. I am glad. They need affection, the poor dogs. And those girls are completely perfect for the task."

"Aye, the poor pups have been through sufficient trials as it is."

Lacey smiled and then replied, "The girls as well. So happy those two have flourished as they have, and that Cook has positively come alive since joining us. Having the responsibility of animals in the home must undoubtedly create memories every family should have."

Turning in his seat, the aging man beamed. "I think you are correct."

"How are their studies going? Will you forgive me for adding the boys to your load now?"

She took a bite of one of the sandwiches and passed the other sandwich over. Hang convention—she could never quite resign herself to eating in front of those around her. Pantersby did not dispute the sandwich, surprisingly. He knew it would do no good. "You know it is something I enjoy immensely. The children are doing very well. I will see how we get on with the boys this weekend. I teach my first class with them on Saturday."

"Thank you." She ate another bite and then pointed at him. "Even though we are still at odds over you not accepting more compensation for your little school, I thank you anyway."

He cleared his throat and expertly brought forth another subject. "Let us discuss Lord Compton again."

"Whatever for? I feel I cannot trust Lord Compton at all. His motives are still singular to his own prize money, and I have never truly felt comfortable amongst the *beau monde*. You know this. You know how hard it is to be amid such people and feel so very alone. Why would I wish to form a union, or even friendship, with a man who only knows such prestige? We are absolutely opposites from one another, he and I. And I believe it is best to keep it that way."

CHAPTER NINE:

That particular lord was at that precise moment debating whether to see the lovely Lady Lamb again, or go to with Terrell to replace his soiled coat. He was currently wearing his green superfine, which was a mite bit better than the gray or navy coats he owned, but still too fine to be worn about town, unless one wanted to be seen. And when did he become so preoccupied with coats, anyhow? Johnson passed over the cravat, and Compton expertly knotted it into a flawless waterfall and then considered himself in the looking glass.

Much too fine for the likes of Lady Lamb's residence. *I will most likely find myself in another dirtied muddle with those puppies.*

At that moment, Terrell rapped upon the door, and Johnson let the man in. "I have another round of invites, my lord. Where do you wish me to put them?" He looked to have at least twenty or thirty.

He turned from the mirror in horror. "Has the *ton* gone mad? What is the meaning of this? Do they honestly believe either I or Lady Lamb will attend a fraction of these? I take it the table is overflowing so you thought to bring them up to me?"

Terrell nodded. "Yes, my lord. It is a very small table, and there are simply too many of them to fit upon it."

"Well then, stuff the whole lot into a pouch of some sort and I will take them to Green Street and solve this with Lady Lamb."

"My lord?"

"Yes? Ought she not to be the one to decide what to do with these copious amounts of invites?" He grinned, suddenly eager to see her again. "I am convinced she finds herself in a similar predicament. This is absurd. Why should I be the only one to be plagued with this nonsense when we are evidently both responsible?"

Terrell cleared his throat as if condescendingly. "Very good, my lord. I will collect them all for you." He bowed and then left with the letters.

"Johnson, does Terrell think I am out of my wits?"

His valet went to collect his Hessians and helped place them on each foot. "Why would you say such a thing?"

Compton took a deep breath. "I cannot quite understand it myself, only that since being in the presence of Lady Ice, I now have become much more conscious of the relationship I have with my staff. I am beginning to care what they think, and it feels … different."

"Your staff?"

"Yes. Now do not look at me like that, or I will most certainly convince myself that you all think I am mad. I am not mad, you know—well, perhaps a little tinged, but not completely. No. However, I do feel a change coming about."

Johnson gave the final tug on the second boot. "Well, that is nothing to shake your head at, my lord. Change can mean a great many surprises."

Compton glanced at the door the butler had departed through. "Yes, but somehow I fear this transformation will strike me to my core." He sat down on the high-backed chair in his dressing room. "She responds so contrary to anyone I have ever met."

He waited for Johnson to say something, but when he did not, he tried again, "Come, man! Are you not inquisitive enough to make conversation with me?"

"Aye, my lord. I am very curious."

"Good!" He beamed and patted the seat next to him.

"But sir, I do not feel comfortable sitting with you."

"Are we to do this again? First Terrell, and now you." He indicated the small boot bench near him. "Then sit there. You work twice as hard as any of the other servants, as you have to put up with my inconsistencies and grumblings."

Tentatively, Johnson sat upon the bench. "I still do not understand what this has to do with anything."

"If Lady Ice can communicate with her servants as if they were acquaintances or colleagues, then I would prefer to hear from you what your thoughts are as well."

"Does she truly sit down with them and converse?"

"It would seem so. As if they were old friends. I have never seen anything of the like."

"How remarkable. If this is true, then I have never heard of another of her class."

Compton shook his head. "How does one remain approachable when it is considered a working relationship at best?"

Johnson scratched at his sideburns. "I have not the faintest notion. I fear it would complicate things dreadfully."

"Lady Lamb does it so carefree. As if it is second nature, and quite easy."

The older man leaned forward. "After all these years, perhaps it was a very good thing she turned you down at the ball."

"How so?"

"Why, because from the moment you noticed her, you have begun to awake out of whatever stupor you have been in."

A flash of irritation made its way through Compton. "I was most certainly not in a stupor."

"Oh, heavens, yes. We have all talked about it through and through. You have been numb for nearly six years or so. Ever since Miss Dappling, you have never been the same."

Miss Dappling? He had not thought of the chit for a couple of years at least. Odd that Johnson would think to bring her up now. And even more peculiar was though he inwardly cringed in anticipation of the sting her name would cause, no sharp pains wounded his heart. Perhaps he was truly over the past. "I cannot imagine what you mean. I have been in high spirits, laughing, larking, dancing... I am in better form than I have been for ages."

"No, my lord." Johnson cleared his throat. "Pardon me, if I speak too frankly. I ought not to express such things around you."

"If you merely being forthright is going to upset me, then perhaps I need to hear it more than I realize," he said, mimicking Terrell's response earlier.

"You have been a mere shell of the man we once knew. The man with passion and dreams and eager to do better in the world."

He thought back to that young naïve lad and looked down, his eyes unconsciously going over his boots. "Those dreams were dreams of a simpleton. Of a boy who thought the world revolved around change, not century-old customs."

"She stole that from you. Do you not remember?"

A vision of the lovely Miss Dappling, all pinky froth and giggles, a young seventeen-year-old girl who would sit for hours and listen to his nineteen-year-old self imagine the world as it ought to be.

"She encouraged you. She made you laugh. Aye, my boy, you were so hopelessly in love with her, there was nothing you would not have done had she asked it of you."

The glee, the hope, the thirst for life and a future. "Yes, I remember."

"When she left, you fell, and you have not had a spark or an ounce of anything to bring you back again."

He thought of Lady Ice's curious ways and gentle smile and complete disregard for any of the rules of society. "Until present."

"Lady Lamb does not bend to convention well, does she?"

Compton gave a short chuckle. "No, she does not."

"It is refreshing?" Johnson asked.

"Yes. Though remarkably so."

"And why is that?"

"I do not know. She is strikingly beautiful, but does not give a fig about beauty. She cares little for the *ton*, and abhors any type of snobbery or class system altogether. It is—she is—I mean to say, she is very mesmerizing."

"And what of the bet at White's?"

He rubbed his lips together and examined the fine shine upon his Hessians. "I do not know. She has every reason to hate me, but I do not feel she is the type to long hate anyone."

"You are complete counterparts."

"Are we?"

"Oh, yes. Even if you were brave enough to consider a match, I would counsel against such a design."

He sighed and ran a hand through his hair. "I do not desire her in that light anyhow, but I am curious now. Why are you set against it?"

Johnson stood and groaned a bit in doing so. Then he turned to Compton and said, "Because if this lady is half the woman I believe her to be, it behooves me to keep her interests at heart. I fear, my lord, that you would very easily crush her, and that would never do. She needs a man who can see and embrace all that she is. One to support her and love her uniqueness, not mock it."

A flash of anger coursed through him. "And you do not feel I can be that person? How low must you think my character to be?"

Johnson met his eye and stood firm. "You have asked for my opinion, my lord, and I have given it. No, I do not feel you can be half the man Lady Lamb needs."

CHAPTER TEN:

Chagrined and more cross than he would have admitted to anyone, Lord Compton drove his curricle to Green Street with a good deal less cheerfulness he had felt an hour before. He was in such deep ruminations over what Johnson had revealed, he succeeded in going past Lady Lamb's house altogether and then had to turn about as he came up to Hyde Park at the end of her street. Botheration! Why the deuce had he attempted the wretched conversation with Johnson anyway? He was positive his valet misunderstood his intentions toward Lady Lamb or he would have never implied such insulting prejudices. Not half the man she needed, indeed! He was twice the man she needed—the lady had no man at all. Was that not proof enough? Thunderation! Vexing toad! He should send the man packing that very night for such preposterous judgements!

He had no one to fault but himself as he became his very own black-hearted villain. Irrefutably, it was a wonder Lady Lamb entertained him at all. And for what outcome was his preposterous, wastrel behavior? Who permits themselves to be concealed behind deep gloom for so long that they literally waste away their own existence?

Compton pulled over about five houses down from Lady Lamb's, removed his top hat, and rubbed his weary face with his hands. This was a beggar's mess. Did he not request the truth, though shocking it may be? Humiliation attacked him in droves as he sat perched upon the seat of his curricle, unexpectedly lonely and forsaken. He had friends enough who delighted in his larks, though recalling their shocked looks at Perceval's ball, when they explained Lady Ice's counter wager, would suggest otherwise. Yet how did one go about redeeming oneself?

Perhaps it was merely a day-by-day approach until one learned how to live again.

Compton drove on and up to Lady Lamb's door with the pouch of invitations. He adjusted his beaver hat, jumped down, put a smile on his face, and was met by Pantersby, who was quick to inform him that his mistress was not at home to visitors at present.

"But why?" he asked determinedly, knowing full well Pantersby merely meant she was not up for entertaining. "I am here to discuss this growing number of invitations and to visit the pups. If she would rather not see me, I understand, but please let me know when would be a better time."

Pantersby bowed and allowed him to step into the vestibule before heading down the long stretch of hallway.

"Oh, very well," he could hear Lady Lamb loudly exclaim. "You might as well send him into the library with us. And fetch more tea. I find I am famished again, and Lord Compton will more than likely eat as well."

The butler returned, and Compton had some difficulty maintaining a straight face as the man properly relayed everything the lady had vociferously announced.

He followed Pantersby into a large library, beautifully
preserved, that had floor-to-ceiling bookshelves all the way
to a large table in the middle of the room. It had scattered
upon it several piles of missives, undoubtedly the same as
those invitations he carried with him. Lady Lamb sat on a
chair in front of it all, shaking her head.

"Look what you have done to me," she exclaimed as
he came in. "This is the chaos I find myself in."

"I would feel sorry for you, but—" He held up his
pouch, opened the thing, and then tilted it so she could see
inside. "I am in the exact same predicament."

"They have been coming in nonstop all day. The post
was bad enough, but now they are being delivered by every
errand boy the *beau monde* keeps. Several are for last-minute
balls and entertainments and such. 'Tis positively
ludicrous."

"I am well aware. It would seem we are the talk of
society"

"Did you expect us to be anything else?" She groaned
and straightened up in her chair. "Pardon me. Please have a
seat. Pantersby will be in with some tea shortly."

He sat down across from her. "It is why I came now.
The last few days have been overwhelming, and I wanted to
know how you would like to go about it."

"Go about what, exactly?"

"Are you willing to attend these events? Or continue
to stay closeted away? Clearly, the hostesses are expecting
us to attend. What say you? I will follow your lead on this."

She pushed a pile toward him. "I am not certain what
to do at present. These are the ones Pantersby assures me I
will want to attend. But as for the others, I doubt I know
anyone and will feel extremely out of place being there.
You understand my disgust of the gabblemongers and

those who fancy themselves able to stare rudely without causing a scene."

He chuckled and met her blue eyes for a moment. Behind their icy resolve, he found a faint uneasiness and fear lurking. His curiosity grew too great. "Why do you despise society so much? You were, I think, not brought up that way. I hear the late viscountess loved to entertain and threw many lavish parties, as well as attending several herself. Even your own brother participates in balls and other grand affairs, and your father was known to show up to several events during the Season. Why is his daughter now so against them?"

"You speak as if you believe something dreadful happened to me." She picked up a missive and flipped it over in her hand, almost as if she were pretending to read it. "Nothing happened."

"And yet?"

She threw the small folded parchment onto the middle of the table. "Bother it. Nothing occurred. Why will you not be satisfied? For that is the truth. Now leave me be."

Compton absentmindedly picked up two or three of the invitations and looked them over nonchalantly. "Seems to be a mighty fine objection for something that never transpired."

"Ooh, you are a troublesome man."

He glanced up and gave an audacious wink.

Lady Ice's pretty lips fell open and then she laughed. In one small, teasing play, the wall was down. Truly, she was not as cold and hard as he had been led to believe.

"Fine. Though it humbles me greatly to share this with anyone, least of all the man who is attempting to get beneath my skin."

"You sound as if I am an insect of sorts."

"Well, are you not?" She had a coy look and blinked, then quickly talked over him before he could protest. "I say nothing happened because it did not. I had my season like any eager girl of sixteen or seventeen, and was as excited as I could imagine for it. My mother insisted on new gowns, which I did not protest, and my father bought me a beautiful all-white mare to prance about on. My dancing slippers matched my gowns, and my hair had been cropped to the latest fashion and my instructor of social graces was hailed to be the greatest in London. I was set. I had even been presented at court in a lavish gown, along with fourteen other young ladies coming out that year. There was a night agreed upon, invitations had been sent, and my coming-out ball was expected to be a mad crush."

"And yet?" he pried.

"And yet, the night of, the nerves that plagued me all day long became fruitless. It would seem I had nothing to be nervous about." She flipped through a few more cards and tossed them aside, and he noticed that her hands were trembling slightly. "A great national disaster of some sort happened four hours before the ball was to begin. My father had been up at Parliament, and several men had broken in and pointed a pistol right at one of the lords. The place exploded with gunshots and powder, and everyone rushed to the grand building. Including my frantically worried mother. And that was that."

His chest tightened as he imagined the beautiful girl with all her hopes and dreams riding on this one moment in her life—the greatest moment she had known until that day—and then ... "I recall that day. It was petrifying. I was not in London at the time, but I remember hearing about it for weeks after. I envision that due to such a deplorable event, no one remembered the ball?"

Jenni James

She shook her head. "My mother and father were so apprehensive with the whole of everything, they came back that night in anxiousness and we all packed our belongings and headed back into the country. Father was adamant that we remain safe and secure until everyone was certain this group of renegades would not attempt to harm their families as well. No one knew to whom they owed such terror. Many assumed it was led by the French, but it could not be proven."

"What did your parents say about the neglected ball?"

She shrugged. "They were in such agitated spirits, I did not have the heart to bring up my own selfishness during the midst of such tragedy."

"So you never said a word? Did they ever recollect it themselves?"

"I do not recall; my mother may have months later. To be fair, she had been so fretful about my father's safety, I do not think it mattered overly much to her."

"And what about the following Season? Was no ball brought up then?"

Her small hands clenched tightly around the folded piece of vellum, and he feared she would crumble it. "I did not attend the following year. My father died."

All of a sudden, he understood much more than what she had revealed. "Your mother never did come out of mourning. She retired from society until her own death two years ago. I have not seen her for ages."

Lady Lamb would not meet his eyes. "Mother needed me at home. She was not well, and I became her companion. Running errands, pouring the tea, seeing to her sewing—all the silliness and quietness of the country."

"Did you never come back up for the Season?"

"In my later years, I kept Betsy on to take care of Mother and accompany my brother, but only for

Parliament, and then I was rushed back home to be with my mother again. By that time, I had lost all the magic town provided and felt quite out of place attending the few events I did—no longer remembering the jigs and dances, nor the names of anyone around me. It was a very hopeless case."

He was surprised to feel the heaviness of her plight resonate so firmly in his chest. "The beautiful bluestocking before me has never had a season."

CHAPTER ELEVEN:

"You do not have to say so in such a manner." Lacey felt her own sad chest tighten in annoyance.

"Like what?" Lord Compton asked.

"As if you are pitying me."

"But I am pitying you. Your tale is very sorrowful. I know of not one gel in your position who would not be jaded by such harsh treatment. To have a mother so full of her own fears and loss to remember that she had a very striking and marriageable daughter waiting for her moment to take the *ton* by storm."

"Oh, bosh. Is that all that matters to you lot? Marriage? Nay, you are mocking me. Enough."

"No, not at all. I am quite serious. For how does one recover when her own mother does not think of her? Of course you would feel put out and not quite the thing when attending the events. And to be constantly alone and overlooked would completely harm any young lady's whims into believing they were not worth the dream to begin with."

"Lord Compton, please stop. You have proven your value as a theatrical master. Perhaps your talents would be put to better use upon the stage."

"No, my dear, I know exactly what my talents shall be used for. I have many gifts that would be considered very advantageous for you."

"Whatever for?"

"To see that you have your coming out, of course!"

Lacey froze as she evaluated his enthusiastic smile and felt her whole body grow taut and gradually turn into stone. He was completely serious. Good gracious, how was she ever to stop him? "Please, I beg of you, break this train of thought instantly. A woman at my age, having a coming out? Why, I would be the laughingstock of the whole of England. 'Tis not even humorous to mention such a thing. I am becoming out of sorts imagining the horrors that would await."

His smile fell. "What of the missed Season? Surely you cannot dream of letting that go as well."

Was he a simpleton? "That fantasy has long gone."

He sighed as Pantersby entered the library with the tea. "What fantasy has long gone, my lady?" the older man asked as he set the large tray near Compton's elbow.

"She will not fathom having her own coming-out ball. Lady Lamb never had one, you see."

"Yes, I did know that." Pantersby looked over at her. "But I cannot imagine she would wish to have one now. She is most certainly not a young miss fresh into her first Season."

"Aye, but that is exactly what she has been saying, Pantersby. She has never had a Season before."

"And you attempt to humiliate her by insisting on one?" the old butler asked.

"Pantersby, please join us and help me talk this nodcock out of such a preposterous idea."

Compton grinned and then watched as though he were fascinated as Pantersby first poured them all tea and then joined them around the table, sitting in the chair nearest her. "You look completely dumbfounded, my lord. Is something on your mind?" she asked him.

"As well he should be speechless," answered Pantersby before he could reply. "I have told you for years now that it is not acceptable for me to be sitting here with you, and of course he is—"

"Oh, heavens!" Lacey sighed, growing more frustrated with each passing moment. "Please do not start this again, and pass the sandwiches as well as a portion of cheese. I see Cook has outdone herself today."

"Very well, my lady," Pantersby replied as he brought her a plate of all she asked for and then made one for himself.

"You can stop looking like that," Lacey said to Compton.

That man blinked and shook his head slightly. "Pardon me. It is merely intriguing to watch you two interact as if you have been the best of friends for many years—or even family."

"Pantersby is my family. I have known him as long as I have known anyone. He was my tutor, and now retired, he answered my advertisement for a butler." She flipped a linen napkin upon her lap. "When I declined, he basically refused to leave or allow any other riffraff to come to my door and apply for the position. Now he does not understand how I simply cannot see him as anything but my tutor, and why I insist on asking his advice and eating with him. For did we not, you and Chull, eat together a good many meals when I was a child? Besides, why would I wish to eat alone when someone as dear to me as a father is in the other room?"

"Would you care for some sandwiches?" Pantersby asked, interrupting her. "It is useless to argue with Lady Lamb—she has made up her own mind. It is better to go along with her outlandish notions and eat. Honestly, these sandwiches are wonderful, and it would be a great pity if you went away hungry merely because Lady Lamb has chosen to be contrary to the rest of the world—at least, that is my opinion on the matter."

"I feel as though I have been completely bamboozled in a madhouse." Compton chuckled. "And thank you, yes. I do not wish to forfeit myself nourishment for anything."

"Hear, hear! Very wise," said the butler as he brushed aside a pile of invites and placed a heaping plate in front of the lord.

After a few bites, Lacey leaned forward and asked, "Now tell me everything that is developing in that head of yours, for I fear I have not heard the last of this 'Season' nonsense."

Compton nodded as he finished one of his sandwiches and then applied a napkin to his lips. "I see these mounds of invites upon this table, and I know there is an equal amount that I have brought as well. It occurs to me that as an intelligent lady, you cannot profess to loathe something you do not even know."

"I fear I discern exactly where you are headed with such a statement," she grumbled with a rueful grin.

"Then you perhaps see how difficult it would be to argue against such flawless logic?"

"There is nothing rational about proposing to go traipsing about amongst the elite, accepting such frivolous offers when you are well aware they are based off the need to be present so others can ascertain which of us is winning the bets."

"Very well. What if I propose another offer altogether?"

"No. One of your schemes has been enough, thank you."

"Nay, listen. Let us attend, say, twenty of these events, and then in exchange, I will remove my bet from White's, forfeiting the whole wager at once."

Pantersby smiled, and Compton pounced. "See? Even Pantersby thinks it a grand idea."

"I would never agree to attend ten such outings, let alone twenty," she responded in scornful disgust.

The butler laughed. "'Tis true, and the genuine motive for why I smiled. Though it does have a ring of fairness to it."

"Fairness? Fairness?" Lacey could feel her temper rising. "That is the whole preposterous point of this—none of it was just. Not once has anything been impartial to me." She looked at Compton. "Ever since you foolishly wagered against me, I have been biased against, and now I am supposed to be grateful that you would blackmail me into attending such disagreeable larks? Have you lost your wits? No, halt. Do not answer that. We can all evidently distinguish the answer."

"Lady Lamb, I beg your pardon. I had no idea my actions would take the turn they have."

"Of course you did not!" she fumed. "You certainly had no thought except for your own wounded pride from the moment you entered White's."

"Actually, it was long before that. In fact, it was a good three days of nursing my shattered ego after you turned me down for the quadrille."

"As if I know how to dance the quadrille, where several dancers form lines and then dance in front of each other. Where one wrong step could potentially not only embarrass me in front of everyone there, or worse, throw the whole movement off! Nay, sir, I do not wish to dance the quadrille with anyone, least of all a monstrous scoundrel who immediately runs to White's and gambles with my name."

"I see." Compton stood up and bowed slightly. "I fear we will always come to heads over this. Forgive me. You are too heated to speak of such at the moment. Would you mind greatly if Pantersby took me to see the puppies and their mama?"

Lacey blinked and then closed her mouth. "Of course. I am certain he would be most happy to show you into the kitchens." She could not help one last jab. "Even though it has a large fire going to prepare dinner tonight, I am fairly positive it will be much cooler in that room than in here, of course. So you are best to run away now."

He nodded his head in acknowledgement and grinned. "I thought so as well."

Irksome man!

CHAPTER TWELVE:

Lacey remained in the library, looking over the infuriating invitations. They were merely sent to make a mockery of them both. It was outrageous to believe she would attend any such folly. Her mother did not raise her to have the Melbourne name bantered about in polite society.

Eventually, Pantersby came back in the room, sat down on the chair he had most recently vacated, and nudged her elbow. "It would not be such a bad thing to at least try to make an appearance at a few, if not more of them."

She glanced into his exhausted eyes and decided now was not the time to release her frustrations on him. "How was Compton? Is he with the dogs now?"

"Yes. Went straight to their box and immediately began to pet and jabber at them. I think he loves those pups."

Lacey took a deep breath and attempted to cool herself. "No doubt. They are adorable." She then worried her lip and looked down at the table. The invites seemed to swim before her. "Am I being unreasonable to dismiss Lord Compton so easily?"

"Unreasonable, no. Not after what you have already been subjected to." He shifted in his seat. "However, had he been anyone else offering to take you around London, someone to guarantee you can discover your way through the throngs and mishaps and all, would you have taken them up on it?"

"At my age? Certainly not."

"Lady Lamb, you are only twenty-five. You are in your prime. What Lord Compton says is correct—it is unfair to spurn something you have never allowed yourself to experience. I say, give the matter some thought. You have a reclusive companion here with Mrs. Crabtree—one who sleeps and reads more than actually protects you, but mayhap she could be prevailed upon to go out and enjoy a bit of society."

She smiled at the thought of the fluttery Mrs. Crabtree being her chaperone at such grand events. Knowing the widowed woman, she would more than likely lap up every bit of it. It would do her a world of good to get out and partake of the life around her.

She had written, answering the call of housekeeper, but Lacey did not have the heart to put such a demanding position upon her. After taking the elderly woman into her home, supplying her with tea, and slowly prying information from her, it did not take long to gather that this woman had once lived in a fine house. She was a poor distant relation of an earl, but after the lady she had been companion for died, she found herself homeless and without work. Lacey had hoped to do without a companion altogether, but did not have the heart to turn the sweet Mrs. Crabtree away. Therefore, without much ado, Lacey had a respectable companion should she ever need her, and Mrs. Crabtree had an easy board.

Nevertheless, to attend balls? Could she actually do such a thing and endure? Lacey closed her eyes and thought back to that young girl who had so many fanciful ideas and dreams. She was astonished she could remember each and every detail of when her coming-out gown arrived a week before the ball. The dizzying excitement as she carried the box up to her room and then the calming reverence as she laid it upon her bed and stared at that box a full ten minutes, imagining the glories inside. She had purposely not called anyone to help her dress and had locked the door. The last thing she desired was for her mother to tell her she could not try on the gown, or any other such trivial nonsense.

Each breath of anticipation revolved around vivid daydreams of the young men and women who would see her arrayed in such splendor as she floated through dance after dance. Her eager hands had shaken as she lovingly touched the paper-covered box and then finally released the twine.

As the lid came off, she carefully peeled back even more paper and held her breath as she pulled out the beautiful gown of light cream silk with its white overlay of intricate lace detailing and seed pearls embroidered throughout. It was by far the most striking and expensive dress she had ever owned. The *modiste* was gracious enough to include a few matching pearl and lace ribbon baubles to adorn her hair.

Very, very gently, she put the dress on and then walked over to the looking glass. She beheld a glorious princess attending her first-ever ball, and her young heart beat in fervent anticipation. How she could be fortunate enough to have the world align so perfectly to allow her these splendors, she would never know. Yet, Lacey could guarantee there was no other seventeen-year-old in all of London who was happier than she was then.

Her brows furrowed in thought as she came back to the present. "Pantersby, I am going to my room for a moment. Can you please catch Lord Compton before he leaves and see that he meets me in the green drawing room? I may wish to speak to him again."

Pantersby looked at her quizzically, but thankfully did not comment as she made her way out of the library and up the stairs to her chambers. Lacey hastily fetched a chair and brought it to the wardrobe. She remembered glancing at a box from her bed, there upon the very top of the thing, behind its fancy carving, and not having a recollection of what it was. The maid clearly had it placed up high to be out of sight. *Could it be?*

Upon the chair, on tiptoe, Lacey reached her hands above her head and found the parcel. Cautiously, she brought it over the carving and down toward her, stepping off the chair as she did so. There it was. The box her coming-out gown had arrived in. Gingerly, she brought it over to the bed, half imagining the gown to be long gone by now, and gasped when she opened it to find her very same dress tucked inside.

Oh, my goodness! It was even more exquisite, and shimmered more elegantly, than she recalled. And it still had the dainty hair baubles as well. In an absurd show of silliness, Lacey swiftly removed her plain muslin gown and slid the cool lace-overlaid cream silk on. Then with great caution, she headed toward the very same mirror as when she was younger and stood transfixed.

There before her was a graceful lady, no longer the lighthearted child she once was, but a fully developed woman, whose unfashionable curves and lines were showcased extremely well in the gown. Much more so than the girl of seventeen had once appreciated. Her eyes sparkled, her cheeks reddened becomingly, and as she brought her hair down and then tucked back up again to allow soft red curls to frame her face, she beheld a delicate angel.

My! How was it that she had seen the same face her whole life and never truly saw the loveliness that she was? Not that it signified—beauty was something someone was gifted with. It held no significance anywhere else except for the exceedingly vain. True character meant and always would mean the most to her.

Pantersby knocked upon her door, snapping her out of her reverie, as he called through it. "Lady Lamb, Lord Compton is awaiting you in the green drawing room."

She hesitated a moment before she answered, "Uh . . . thank you, Pantersby." And bravely opened the door.

The old man's eyes shown mistily as he met hers, and they—neither of them—spoke for a thoughtfully long minute.

Was this not the stupidest thing she had ever done? The folly of a wishful moment. Though she did not speak the words out loud, he answered them.

"Viscountess Melbourne, my littlest Miss Lacey Lamb, if I could have but one wish for you, it would be that my lady would wear this gown and prove she is every bit as worthy to hold her title as the rest of the *Ton*." He broke all rules and clutched her hands to his chest, his eyes swimming. "My dear, you look so much like your cherished mother, and it is time society remembers you both."

CHAPTER THIRTEEN:

Compton stood up as Lady Lamb entered the room in her very plain brown dress and was surprised to perceive a slight air of change about her.

"Forgive me for keeping you waiting," she said as she approached him, both hands out.

He clasped her hands and stood stunned for a moment. "It was nothing. Pantersby said you wished to speak to me?" Compton had learned long ago never to assume what a lady was thinking or how she was about to react during any situation. To do so would lead his thoughts on a merry chase, and it would all come to naught when she actually spoke. Therefore, Compton had been enjoying himself quite easily, pondering over the great improvement in the puppies for the quarter of an hour it took for Lady Lamb to join him.

She was all smiles as she sat back down and asked him to sit as well, her whole countenance assuming a refreshing quality he had never recognized in her before. And then she spoke, and entirely flummoxed him.

"You were correct. I do not know why I have become such an old gudgeon of late, but I certainly wanted to beg your pardon and confess that I have had a change of heart. After thinking it through for some minutes, I acknowledge, though still cautious, that there is a new eagerness that abides within me. Lord Compton, I fear I would like to attend some of the events that have been presented to us both. Mind you, I do not believe my attitudes of society will change, only that I have never partaken in this sort of adventure, and I have a mind to do so now." Then she smiled. That smile could slay the hearts of a thousand men, if she only but knew it. However, her ease and naturalness were her charm.

The effortlessness of merely being, and knowing her own purpose and direction—she wore those incredible attributes well, and many a man, or lord, would be foolish indeed not to see the power her artlessness could have over them.

"I am all astonishment, my dear. In fact, I had quite resigned my fate to go through some of these galas on my own, with only my friends' merriment and jests at my failed attempts to woo you, as my companions."

"They will all speak of us."

"Of course, but we will not care a jot."

"We will not?"

"No. Indeed, though they will be whispering behind their fans, we will be holding our heads high and laughing at the lot of them."

"Good gracious. Why would we ever do that?"

He leaned forward. "Because," he whispered, despite Pantersby's frown at such familiarity, "we will know the truth."

Lady Lamb mimicked him and leaned forward too, their faces merely inches apart. "And what is that?" she whispered back.

His mouth formed his most dashing grin as his gaze caught her twinkling eyes. "Why, that we have formed a truce, and neither of us could give one fig about the wagers."

She stared at him blankly, and then recognition dawned. "Of course. They are all expecting us to be fighting horrendously or wooing each other, are they not?"

"Precisely. And when we are doing neither, except perhaps enjoying their antics to see who has the most outrageous rumor about, we shall giggle about them quite justly."

"But it is wise to appear to be in each other's company? Would it not be best if we did not speak at all?"

"After I have been seen coming to and from your house more than once? I do not think it signifies whether we are speaking together or not."

Her grin matched his, and she chuckled. "Very well. I will be present at five of the same occasions that you deem worthy enough to attend."

"I thought I said twenty such events."

"Twenty? No. I would go mad if I had to prance about at twenty soirees. It would certainly drive me to an early grave."

He shook his head, but replied, "Then let us come to a compromise. Shall we make it ten, then? You cannot truly say you have lived through a Season unless you essentially attend enough gatherings to make it seem real."

"Very well. I shall attend eight, though I refuse to budge past that number."

There was nothing he wished to do more than kiss the smirk off the delectable minx's countenance. Compton

[77]

cleared his throat and put his hand out. "Done. We shall appear at eight gatherings together, and you, my dear, despite the lack of a coming-out ball, shall have your very first Season."

* * *

Much later that night, long after Lord Compton had returned home, Lacey made her way down to the cozy kitchens. He and Lacey had affably debated over whose invitations would be most beneficial to attend, and whose would not. She had been adamant that they appear at those events whose hosts were kind and not known for being overly gossipy, as well those who followed the political circles. Compton wanted to attend gatherings he knew would not be a complete bore, or waste of his time—such as Lady Pellington's annual garden tea party, which always sounded lovely, but more often than not was a drizzled-upon mess of mud and boring poetry and sonnet readings.

Lacey smiled at the memory of his antics as he described the most tedious of afternoons spent amongst the *ton* and those she should avoid at all costs. As it was, they were able to come up with a quite respectable list of eight. Before she could change her mind, Pantersby and Compton both saw that she sent her acceptance letters immediately.

Now, as she approached the box of puppies and their mama, she had begun to have second—nay, fifth or sixth thoughts. She wrapped her shawl tightly around her dressing gown and sat down on a small rug next to the wooden box. The oil lamp above her on the table glowed gently upon the sleeping brood.

Mama was doing so much better now. Her breathing was even, and though she was still very thin, Lacey could feel her coat thickening and life coming back to the dear girl. "And how do you like your new home?" she asked as she reached in and rubbed the top of her head. Mama looked up and whimpered slightly, allowing Lacey to pet beneath her jowl and scratch her neck. "Your babies are doing wonderfully," she whispered so as not to wake the fluffy lumps. "You are a good mother. Has anyone thought to tell you what a noble mama you are?" Her eyes met those of the dog, and she felt a sudden warmth come over her. It was if the animal discerned what she was conveying to her.

"You are so very brave as well. To have your puppies in Hyde Park, of all places, and then to hope and pray someone would come along and save them—is that what you wished for? Do animals wish for things? I often believe my horses do. They are particularly wishful when I bring a carrot or sugar cube for them." She giggled quietly. "The rascals will nudge and bump and snort into me until I give in and offer them their treat."

Suddenly, her smile faded. "I wish I were as brave as you. I wish the world was as perfect as I once believed it was, but it is not. Of course you know this, do you not? Left all alone to raise pups, unable to fend for yourself from lack of nutrients. Yet Pantersby has determined that you will come out of it. He seems to think I will come out of it as well. I do not know what he expects—perhaps for me to wake up one morning and be whole and cheerful and not quite so bitter about those my mother and father treasured so dearly."

She gasped. Her hand went straight to her mouth, and her eyes widened. Was that the greatest of her worries? Was that what concerned her so very much? Lacey shifted slightly and stared into the box, but no longer saw the sweet family inside. Instead, her eyes began to swim with tears at the recollection of her mother—her dearest, sweetest mother. The woman who had not a thought for herself over a friend or loved one. Viscountess Melbourne continuously threw large parties and grand affairs so her friends could meet and enjoy themselves. For how many a young girl had she hosted a coming-out gala in the London mansion? How many musicals had she hosted when she discovered a new operatic singer or musician she wanted to assist into society? Mother even had Cook prepare some nice dessert for those who were ill, and one of the footmen, or even herself at times, would take the confection round to her friend to cheer her up.

Even in the country, life would remain blissful and busy, consoling those around her and finding ways to beat the gray England gloom. Yet on the days when her mother became distraught over the loss of her husband, no one came to uplift her. No one brought over a gift or took her out of the house on an escapade or two. Nay, she stayed as much of a recluse and the opposite of what she once was until her death. Had but just one friend remembered her and brightened her day with a smallish bit of gossip, Lacey was convinced her mother's life would have perhaps lasted years longer. However, sadly, all those joyous people in her life continued on with their frivolities, and Lacey began to wonder if any of them ever gave her mother another thought.

The fickleness of those in society was a lesson Lacey would much rather never had to learn. And yet, she sighed and wiped at her tears, she would be keeping an appointment with the *modiste* tomorrow noon. For what? To be brought into this circle of people who would turn their backs on her the moment she was wont to need them?

"Shh, now. Are you crying, Lady Lacey?"

Lacey turned when she heard the old housekeeper's voice. "I am afraid you have caught me, Mrs. Chull."

The woman knelt down upon the rug next to her and placed an arm around her shoulders, her red-and-white-striped dressing gown pooling about her as she lowered herself. "What is it that ails ye, my lady?"

Lacey leaned into her shoulder and closed her eyes. How many moments had she experienced this very same thing when she was a little girl and Mrs. Chull was her nurse? "I am feeling very alone right now, I suppose."

"Missing your mama?"

Lacey nodded. "Dreadfully."

"She was a good woman. She assisted so many in society."

"Yes, she did."

Mrs. Chull lovingly squeezed Lacey's shoulder and said softly, "You are a respectable woman too, and I daresay even more thoughtful and more benevolent than your mother."

"No. Do not say so. I fear it would be impossible to be thought of in such a light."

Ever so slowly, the old nurse-turned-housekeeper began to rock Lacey. "But you already are. All of us who know you see the greatness that is there. You change worlds, dear. And change lives. Lives that matter to so many more people than your mother saw."

"Whatever do you mean?"

Mrs. Chull took a deep breath and kissed her forehead as if she were a little child. "Why, you see the servants, too. Your mother, though kindness in every bit of her nature, had been worried about those left out of society. Those who needed a compassionate word, or something to lift their spirits, whilst you—you see the lost, scared souls society does not. Take me, for instance."

Lacey pulled back. "You? Mrs. Chull, you know very well I refuse to acknowledge anything negative you have to say about yourself. You have and always will be my nurse, and that is the end of that."

"Even after you grew up? Even after your mother released me from my duties and you pleaded to her to let me stay on? Do you not remember how you found me fretting over where I would go once I was released? And how you plucked up the courage at seventeen to tell your parents you simply could not do without me? It was the most humiliating, humbling, most grateful experience of my life, knowing full well there was no need for me, and yet you could not bear to think of me alone, without family."

She shook her head. "Nonsense. It is you who have helped me. Remember, you are my housekeeper nowadays. Without your help, I would have a mere fraction of the time I do now. You run this home with a sharp eye, and I am and will forever be in your debt."

The older woman smiled and sat up straighter. "Well, I do keep a mighty fine house for you—it is no wonder I am given such a grand task."

"My only regret is that I have brought you lower in the working class." She sighed. "Yet neither you nor Pantersby would hear of anything else."

"Of course not, my dear! After all you have done, when you needed assistance, we effortlessly stepped into our new roles."

Lacey was never easy with compliments, but Mrs. Chull, in her own roundabout way, knew precisely how to keep her out of the doldrums and focus on the present. "Thank you. And thank you especially for putting up with my oddities and accommodating whatever new urchin I have fetched home without batting an eyelash."

She chortled and tucked Lacey in tight once more. "There has never been a dull day with you as mistress, that is for sure!"

CHAPTER FOURTEEN:

The next day, before meeting Hamson and Atten at Tattersall's, Compton stopped by Green Street.

"Lady Lamb is not in." Pantersby met him at the door.

"That is fine. I am not here to visit her ladyship anyway." He grinned and pulled a wrapped package from under his arm. "I have come to see the puppies and I have a gift for their mama, as you can perceive."

"A present?"

"Yes. My cook has been thoughtful enough to save a bag of bones and scraps for the darling. Now may I invade your kitchens once more and surprise her?"

"Most certainly. I cannot imagine Lady Lamb taking offense at such a wonderful gesture." He moved back and allowed Compton into the vestibule as he shut the door. "And the little one will surely be happy to have your gifts."

"How are all the pups today?"

"Good, good! Night and day compared to what they looked like when you found them, my lord."

"I am certain much of that has to do with this household and all those who look after the lot. Thank you for allowing me to trespass and leave them in your care. You are benevolent indeed."

These pleasantries and many more were expressed as the two gentlemen made their way into the kitchens. Once again, Compton was taken by the stature and ease the butler presented, and he was reminded of what Lady Lamb had said earlier about Pantersby being her retired tutor who then answered her call for a butler.

"You must be a very remarkable man to have taken on this role in Lady Lamb's house after being her tutor for so many years before. Has it been difficult?"

"I beg your pardon, my lord. No, it is not demanding. Lady Lamb is not the sort to make anything more problematic than it needs to be."

He found that hard to believe. "I did not mean to set your back up, Pantersby. I was merely curious what it was like for you. Forgive my impertinence." Compton bent down to the box, determined to alter the flow of conversation. "Well, hello there. How are you this fine day?" The improved dog wagged her tail, but remained lying down, her nuzzling puppies taking advantage of her position and nursing their mighty hearts out. He opened the package, dangled a small piece of meat, and watched, satisfied, as Mama reached her neck for it and snatched it hastily from his fingertips.

"Well done, you. You are growing much healthier each day."

"Aye, she is. She even made it up and walked about the kitchen a step or two this morning. We were all in excitement, seeing her so willing to begin to explore and give her body a bit of exercise."

"Have you come up with a name for her yet?"

"No. Lady Lamb has left that honor to you, my lord. Though we have all fiddled about with different ones over her time here, she has said you have found her, so therefore, you name her."

"Well, I had no idea my discovering them held such prestige as this." Compton cleared his throat. "Her coat seems to be a nice ginger color." He thought a moment and then said, "What if we called her 'Ginger' or 'Cinnamon'? Would that be a decent alternative to simply 'Mama'? Or what about 'Nutmeg'?"

"That last one is certainly unique, my lord."

"And amusing! I like it. Nutmeg. 'Tis the most perfect name for a dog. And now, please allow your staff and Lady Lamb to name the rest. I could never come up with them all. As her household will be acquainted with their personalities better than anyone else who comes to see them, I would be honored if you would select them."

"Well, thank you, my lord. I know a couple of girls who would be delighted to hear this news."

Nutmeg wagged her tail and nudged into Lord Compton's hands, just as his horses did. He stayed and petted her a little longer, feeding her tidbits before rising and leaving the rest of the odds and ends of meat and bones with Cook.

"Nutmeg will be greatly spoiled, my lord," the cook babbled as she bobbed a curtsy.

"As she should be. You have done wonders with her and the pups." He gave a short nod. "Thank you for all you have done."

"Oh! 'Tis not only me, my lord." Cook flushed. "Why, the girls, Mrs. Chull, the housekeeper, the footman, and Lady Lamb—why, we have all taken to them. They have brought so much life and gaiety to this kitchen, it has been a dream to have such a sweet group to look after."

"That is very glad news to hear. I was half worried you would all wish me to Hades for parting with them."

"Nay! We would never consider such a thing."

Compton tilted his head, and when curiosity took hold, he asked her quite abruptly, "How did you meet Lady Lamb? Have you known her all her life as well?"

He gathered a look of amazement between the butler and the cook.

"Forgive my manners. Am I intruding again? Your relationship and lifestyles fascinate me. It is surprising to see such easiness between nobility and staff, and it is merely nosiness that drives this impropriety of mine."

Cook waved him off. "I'm proud to tell ye how's I met the young lady, though 'tis astoundin' to hear someone wonder about it. Me and my lil' daughters were alone on the streets. My husband was not the kindest of men and became quite ill on drink usually. The night he died, we'd managed to escape the house and run for our lives. My daughters were only four and five at the time. We were unaided and rightly scared. I had no notion of where to go, or what to do—only that my sweeties and I were as protected as I could make us. It was two days later when Lady Lamb stopped her glorious coach in front of us. I was tremblin' somethin' severe, but she was kind and asked if'n I needed assistance. Grateful I was for the help. We climbed into that coach over a year ago, and we have never been more happy."

"And you became her cook straightaway?"

"Oh, no! First I spent months learning all the fancy skills and meals with Mrs. Black, the other cook in the country, while my lil' ones played with the servants' children. Mrs. Black has since retired and lives in a cottage on that grand estate now. The country house is beyond beautiful, but when we moved up here, it was like a dream come true. To be in such a fancy house in the middle of London—on Green Street, no less—and me being the one what's prepares all the meals. A year ago when I was sitting, scared out of my wits, on a small piece of grass prayin' in my heart for something good to happen to us, I would never have imagined this."

She brushed at her skirts. "This dress and apron are made of finer fabrics than anythin' I have ever worn before in my life."

"Mama! Mama!" A little girl with braids and bows and a white pinafore came bounding into the kitchen and straight for the cook's legs. The woman pitched forward as her daughter clung to her. "You haf ta see the puppy," the little girl exclaimed.

"Mary, please curtsy to Lord Compton. He's the one the puppies belong to."

Her face lit up with the most adorable grin. "'Twas you?" She took a step back and then asked very reverently, her eyes wide, "Are you a prince?"

He gave out a surprise chuckle and knelt beside her. "No, but I have met him. And I think it is the nicest compliment you could give someone."

Pantersby began to cough. Clearly, he knew the prince was not the most attractive of men.

"You are very han'some," Mary said. "Are you going ta marry La-ly Lamb?"

"Mary!" The cook grabbed her daughter and pulled her away from Lord Compton. "You do not ask such things of his lordship."

"Why?"

"It is fine." Compton stood back up and grinned, but had no idea how to answer the question. He turned to Pantersby and nudged him in the ribs. "I take it you have met the prince too, before your tutoring days?"

"We all have, Lord Compton," Lady Lamb said as she stepped into the kitchen. "Prince Regent stayed with us in the country many times when I was a girl, and once or twice since my parents have passed on. When my brother is in residence, he has stayed again at the estate."

"Hello, Lady Lamb. I did not know you were home." Compton held his breath and wondered how long she had been there, and what exactly she had overheard.

Mary ran to her and threw her arms all the way around Lacey's legs. "You are backed! You are backed! Come see the puppies! One has her eyes open. You haf ta see!"

CHAPTER FIFTEEN:

Once Compton finally approached Tattersall's, Lord Hamson and Lord Atten were on the west side, rambling out with the new pair of matched horseflesh for Atten's travelling coach.

"You have purchased them without me," he called out as he drew near to the two men.

"We had quite given up on you, old man!" Atten greeted him with a tip of his fine beaver. "Why, we waited in excess of half an hour before heading in."

"'Tis true." Hamson lightly patted the rump of the white horse nearest. "Did you perchance become lost on your way over?"

Compton shrugged. "As lost as one can find himself on Green Street."

Both men gaped at him, and then Atten began to grin. "Out with it! Lady Ice still allows you to show your face around there?"

"What larks have you been up to in that department?" Hamson chimed in. "Tell me, are you as much in love with her as I think?"

"Bah. I am not in love with her at all." He grimaced as convincingly as he could.

Hamson winked. "As of yet. Nevertheless, there is still time."

"Beautiful pair." Compton attempted to change the subject and rubbed the neck of the large horse to his left. "When you said Tat's had such a pair, I did not truly believe you meant of this caliber."

"They are stunning," Hamson agreed.

"And they will look smashing pulling my new black coach, do you not think so?" Atten smugly boasted.

"Yes, they will look quite magnificent."

"Not as magnificent as finally seeing you and Lady Ice together." Hamson laughed. "Now, when will such an occurrence take place? You must tell us, man!"

"Wednesday week." Compton did not meet either of his friends' eye.

"Do you mean the ball at the Stanthorpes' house?" Atten's jaw dropped. "And however did you manage to get Lady Ice to accept such an invitation?"

"It was much easier than anyone would think, really. I only mentioned that Lord Stanthorpe was the Speaker of the House for Parliament. She wrote an acceptance letter instantaneously."

Hamson shook his head. "I hear they have a superb garden to walk in at night."

Were they attempting to see the lady compromised? "I would not care if there were eight such gardens. You can guarantee I will not be escorting Lady Lamb out into any of them."

"So he says at present," Atten crowed. "Mark my words, those cold lips of hers will be ripe for kissing by and by."

"She does not have cold lips." For no reason at all, Compton seemed to be losing his patience. "Nor is any part of her made of ice. In fact, she is most undeniably one of the warmest creatures I have ever beheld." Compton glanced up to catch the raised eyebrows of each of the men. "And you can, both of you, bring those looks back to normal, for there is nothing between the lady and I that was not there a sennight ago, I assure you."

Hamson mockingly displayed a hideous sing-songy voice to mimic him. "Except she is the warmest creature I have ever beheld."

"'Tis true, she is very sincere and benevolent and considerate and generous. Indeed, she a paragon among women."

"And yet when she is attending functions, she stands around with her uncomfortable expressions, and one can tell she wishes herself miles away." Lord Atten shook his head. "Her face is extremely pretty, so it is a great pity she is so ill-favored among society."

Compton's irritation was only increasing. "Enough. She is unlike any woman I have ever known, and I will not allow either of you to mock her, not privately nor publicly."

Atten gestured for his footmen to take the horses and then patted Compton on the back. "Never seen you in such a state, old man. We were merely teasing, nothing vicious."

"I do not like it."

"That we can see!" Hamson was clearly smirking himself out of a chuckle.

"I will denounce you both as fools." Compton tugged on his suit coat and took a deep breath to calm his ire.

Jenni James

"And why is that?" Atten asked. "What has gotten in you? If I did not know better, I would say you are presently deep in it with the gel. Lady Ice could not have altered you so effortlessly."

Compton clenched his fists. It was the deuced use of the word "ice" that was triggering this intense reaction from him. The worst of it was that it was his own fault. He was the one who had come up with the thoughtless name in the first place. "I beg of you not to refer to the Viscountess Melbourne as Lady Ice again."

"So that is what love appears to be?" Hamson retorted.

"I do not know what love is, but I understand respect." Compton moved away from them both. "I believe she has had a hard time of it. The tragedy at Parliament seven or eight years prior has much to do with her present state."

"Fascinating." Atten grinned and tugged on Compton's shoulder, bringing him back. "Come, man, tell us what has happened. What has caused you to have your back up in this manner? Surely there is something in her that has brought this all out. Will you share with us?"

Compton shook his head and glanced down at his shiny boots. "She is intriguing and wholly altogether so unique, I am at a loss for words how to describe her." He looked at him. "I am certain she is not in love with me. If fact, I doubt she feels anything toward me—not because she is cold and unfeeling, but because her need for a man who truly understands her heart far outweighs anything else."

"Whatever could you mean by such a statement? You make it seems as if she belongs in bedlam," Hamson asked, his grin turning into a look of chagrin.

"Nay. Only that she cares for others unlike any of our ilk do." Compton nodded toward Tattersall's. "She is an heiress and could easily buy every bit of horseflesh here—nay, the whole lane of shops could be hers, if she chooses. But instead, from what I have gathered, she spends her time and wealth helping the unfortunate." He glanced toward the road. "Her staff is full of those who have retired, or London beggars she has picked up off the streets. She educates them, I assume she supplies them with a much handsomer wage than any of us would consider, and she clothes them in extremely fine linens."

"What nonsense is this?" Hamson scowled. "Perhaps she *should* be considered a bedlamite. Why? To put oneself in such danger, to entrust your very staff, those who walk willy-nilly through your home, with riff-raff?"

"They love her so. To them she is their savior, the most benevolent woman they know."

Atten shook his head. "And this appears to work in her favor?"

Compton folded his arms. "Aye. They are her friends. They are like family. They would do anything for her. Now, you name me one heiress you know who is half as sympathetic and impartial to those she meets." He looked back at their perplexed faces. "She is not ice—no, anything but. It would seem it is society that is icy. She is merely living as she sees fit without being tied to the dictates of society. Her rules, her abilities, and her example—all of that which is preached among the radical reform groups of England is already her motto."

"Then why buy a stately home on Green Street if she is such a paragon among the poor?" Atten smirked.

"Probably so she has a home large enough to house as much staff as possible. It is not for me to point out the hypocrisy as you so easily do. No, it is for me to rejoice and marvel at the humanity she displays, and the courage she so boldly uses to defy everything she has been taught and grown up to believe. To see past the grime to the healing balm of love and a place of worth."

Hamson chuckled. "Say what you will, my friend, but I have never seen a man so fully dedicated to the aspect of love as you are. The question should not be, are you in love? No, the question must most vehemently be, how are you going to gain her love in return?"

CHAPTER SIXTEEN:

One week later, and Mrs. Crabtree, Lacey's companion for the evening, clapped her white-gloved hands excitedly as Lacey walked toward her from the dressing room. "Splendid! You look so very pretty, Lady Lamb. Why, I have never envisioned such loveliness in my life."

"You are too kind," Lacey said as she attempted to keep her face cool from the blush that was even now threatening to rise. The styles had not changed overly much since her coming out, so with the help of her abigail and an easy tuck of the sleeves and a tiny bit lowering of the gold sash about her waist, anyone could be fooled into believing the gown to be new and not the nearly the eight years old that it was. The exhilaration of her feelings the last time she attempted to wear the gown were long gone. In its place was an overwhelming sense of apprehension and dread.

Her palms sweated appallingly beneath her long gloves. Her heart stuttered, and her stomach had felt as though it had sunk to her knees. Why did she ever agree to such a farce? Let alone eight of them? She had no place in the *ton,* no reason to show her face other than to be mocked and gossiped about.

"You look beautiful as well, Mrs. Crabtree. Your new gown turned out perfectly. The light blue accents your eyes nicely," Lacey said as she smiled to hide her fears. "And a lovely fan you have as well."

"Why, thank you." The older woman chortled as she brushed at her gown and then flipped open the fan. "This was the trinket I was given by my father for my sixteenth birthday. I am in all excitement to be using it at such a grand occasion tonight."

"Yes, the Stanthorpes' ball will be just the thing." She smiled weakly and squared her shoulders. "Shall we go?"

"Yes! I cannot wait for you to take the *ton* by storm."

Apart from the four other times she had been introduced and included into society by her brother or his wife, she knew that the only storm she would be causing was the bitter tempest of gossip. It was one thing to know this fact and stay away. It was quite another to jump headlong into the fray. *Whatever have I gotten myself into?* she thought as she slowly began to descend the stairs after a much-recovered Mrs. Crabtree.

"I am so happy to see you are much more the thing now, and you are feeling well." Such a pity. Heaven knew what she would give for the excuse that her chaperone was ill now. 'Twas not fair.

"Thank you," Mrs. Crabtree chimed as her feet touched the bottom step. "I would not have missed this ball for the world."

Pantersby came to wish them well, and Chull gave her a rather unexpected embrace. "Your mama would be so proud of you right now," she whispered in her ear. "I know this is not your favorite outing, but you look exceptionally fine, and these are friends of your family. Let yourself bloom, my little one. It is time."

No, it was most definitely *not* time. Lacey's acknowledgements and parting words were a blur of agitated nerves. When at long last she could not hide inside her home a moment longer, she found herself and a chattering Mrs. Crabtree entering the coach.

Blindly, she pulled the curtain back and watched the world blur past. Each breath was labored and drowned out the hum of the incessant need Mrs. Crabtree had to gush about this or that along the way. Once the coach halted in front of the Stanthorpes', her hands held on to the seat, refusing to allow her body to budge a centimeter. However, her companion was more than eager, and lightly removed herself from the coach with the help of a footman and then looked expectantly at Lacey, all babbling stopped.

The footman presented his gloved hand to Lacey, and at that moment, she wanted to bang the door shut and tell the driver to head home. Yet, with the expectancy in Mrs. Crabtree and the awaiting hand, Lacey finally drummed up the courage, held her hand out for the footman, and stepped out of the coach. Her eyes met that of the boy David she had saved along with his younger brother.

"Lady Lamb, you will do well."

She was a bit taken aback to see the compassion on his features. Did this young lad know how painful this was for her?

"There is not one of them that willn't fall in love with you by the time the night is through. Beggin' your pardon, my lady, but you look an angel."

He meant it kindly, but his words alarmed her more than helped. "Thank you, David."

The next thing she could recall was being received by her hostess, Lady Stanthorpe, a small-framed woman with dark hair and merry eyes, and her husband, Lord Stanthorpe, Earl of Stanthorpe and Speaker of the House of Parliament. "Welcome, Lady Lamb. It is so nice to see you."

"My pleasure," she responded with a short curtsy, a little in awe at seeing the handsome older general so close. When the couple turned their attention to her companion, Lacey started at her oversight. "Forgive me. This is Mrs. Crabtree."

That lady was all smiles and gushing politeness as she dipped a pretty curtsy. Then she followed Lacey down the hall toward the room with doors flung wide open and the hum of the prattling of society floating out to greet all those attending.

Mrs. Crabtree could barely contain her excitement as they approached the entrance of the grand room. Thankfully, several others were standing about, and they were not noticed easily at first. Lacey gathered her wits around her, and they stood a bit to the side to take in their surroundings. There were so many people. So many that a great part of her wanted to pick up her skirts and dash from the room.

"Lady Lamb, there are two seats just there. Shall we sit?" asked Mrs. Crabtree as those closest to them tittered to a silence at the loud mention of her name.

Lacey met several eyes watching her intently as she looked to her left and right. Her heart clenched, and fear began to replace rational thought. Then the fans swooshed open and went up as they fluttered to cover the gabblemongers' tales. She looked frantically toward the seats Mrs. Crabtree indicated. In a matter of seconds, to her horror, the women behind fans seemed to travel from one person to the next, sharing their gossip, down both sides of the long ballroom.

Hang Compton and his ridiculous notions. Forget Mrs. Crabtree's joys—no one should force themselves to endure such as this. Lacey had to leave that moment. *Nothing is worth this. Nothing.*

She quickly retraced her steps and walked back into the large hallway. In her haste, she was ashamed to admit she had quite left Mrs. Crabtree all alone, but when the senses explode as hers had, one could not be held too accountable for their actions.

"Lady Lamb, wait a moment." It was Compton, she could tell the instant he spoke, but she did not want to halt to find him. As politely as possible, she began to weave her way through those coming down the hall to head past her hosts and toward the front door when all at once, she felt a sharp tug upon her elbow. Without further ado, she was whirled into a side room, a smallish parlor, and the door snapped shut.

CHAPTER SEVENTEEN:

"Compton, allow me to leave at once." She was too apprehensive to be trifled with. Her vision blurred from anxiety and stress, and she did not turn around to face him lest he see the worry upon her features.

"Not until you reveal what ails you." He was nearer to her than she thought. His deep voice must have been less than forty centimeters away. "Come now, what has happened? Who has caused this panic? Tell me this instant, and I will have them removed from the ball directly."

She looked down and fiddled with the fingers of her gloves, nervously plucking at the tips of them. How could she explain? Each anxious breath was forced from her. "It was no one in particular and everyone all at once. They were all speaking of me and I could not experience their gawking another moment longer, so I rushed from the room. It was a mistake to come here. Forgive me."

"Lady Lamb," he persisted gently. She felt one tentative hand touch her arm and very slowly turn her around and tuck her right into the folds of his pristine cravat. "You cannot mean to hurry off before the night has begun."

It felt so peculiar to have his arms most improperly wrapped around her and to be close enough to feel the starched folds pressed into her cheek. His familiarity with her person could not be borne. "Lord Compton, if you do not release me this instant, I will have your guts for garters."

Compton chuckled in her ear, and that small sound managed to wind its way shuddering down her spine. "Oh, how I have missed you. At least you have some fighting spirit left within that heart of yours."

The intolerable man! She pushed against him, and he let her go. "How can you pine for someone you do not know? You do not miss me any more than you miss a stone in your shoe, so halt this nonsense at once. Is it not dreadful enough that you have closeted yourself with me in this parlor with the door closed?"

His eyes went wide, and he had the audacity to laugh as he bowed before her. "Forgive me, Lady Lamb, but it would seem I have compromised you." And then the buffoon knelt upon one knee and reach for her fingers. His mischief knew no bounds as he cleared his throat and said, "I fear I must ask for your hand in marriage at once."

"Get up! What if someone were to come in here and find you thus?" She tugged at his hands. "Nonsense. Of all the outlandish things. You and I both know I have not been compromised. You were merely comforting a friend is all. Now stop this tomfoolery and behave as a gentleman ought."

His chuckles echoed through the small room as he straightened up. "You know I could not resist," he said as he brushed at his coattails. Then their eyes met, and he inhaled slowly as his teasing smile dropped. Lacey had no idea what he saw, but his manner changed completely.

"My dear." He reached up and removed an errant curl from her cheek. "I was not myself just now. Forgive me, and please accept my apologies for the cruelties of the *ton*. I am a monster to expect you to enjoy such belittling tripe as they have no doubt provided. You were correct all along. It is the same everywhere we go in society—we all do speak about each other."

Her voice shook as she admitted, "I am not much in the habit of speaking of another person in such a light— and certainly not publicly, and whilst they are in the same room as I."

"It is because your soul is kinder than ours."

She shook her head, for she felt anything but kind at the moment.

"Come, can I convince you to appear on my arm? We only need to dance a set or two."

"At what cost? Is this another part of the wager I know nothing of? To have me dancing at the balls with you?"

"Of course not! No, this is for you, Lady Lamb."

"What do you mean?"

"You dancing with me proves that their hurtful ways do not touch you, that you are above such disrespect. As well as verifying yourself to be the one winning the wager." He stepped back. "Believe me when I say, I have the most to lose with these actions, and it will be my name spread about so shamefully. I see your reaction to these words— you do not believe me, do you?" He gave a rueful smile and continued. "Even now, I am being mocked by my closest associates. They have noticed a great change in me—one I am not quite willing to acknowledge. However, if my closest friends notice it, what is stopping the rest of the elite?"

"What are you speaking of? These riddles demonstrate that all of this is gibberish and should be wholly avoided."

His eyes captured hers again, and her breath caught in her throat. He was growing to care for her, and he did not bother to hide such a fact. Those orbs of his tugged and pulled and revealed much more than she was willing to believe.

"You are a fool to see me in such a light," she whispered tersely.

He nodded and shuttered those eyes from her. His preposterously long, dark lashes fanned his cheeks and then looked back up once more, this time a bit more distant than before. "I cannot help being irrational then, for no matter what I do, no matter what I tell myself, your goodness comes to mind, and it is all I concentrate on. There is such a joy and ease about you." He took a deep breath. "However, I did not come to make you uncomfortable. I promise I will not be begging for your hand—not even in earnest."

Suddenly, she was very weary. "Why are we here, then?"

"For you to feel loved. Merely that. To enjoy and be welcomed for a night. And though I have been decidedly unkind in not pointing out how lovely you look this evening, let me please rectify that oversight immediately, for you are an unbelievable, magnificent fairy in a gown I could have never imagined or thought of before. It is exceptional, and I truly believe you may be the most beautiful creature to have ever graced the Stanthorpes' ballroom."

She grinned and glanced up toward the ceiling. "If we were anywhere else, I would whack you senseless for such fanciful words."

"Then it is perhaps best that we are not anywhere else."

He took a step forward, and it was truly the first time she noticed their differences in size. Why, her head merely came below his shoulder. If he was not the most irritating man in all of London, she would even go so far as to call him handsome—remarkably so. But it was his manner of enjoying larks a bit too freely that would always unsettle her.

"The music has started. Lady Lamb, could I persuade you to throw me to the gossiping wolves and dance the set?"

It was those blasted eyes. They pried and questioned and were framed by the face of a handsome devil. Heaven knew she should run to her coach and leave the premises straightaway when all of a sudden, she remembered dear Mrs. Crabtree! "My companion! Er, yes. Let us go in at once and look for her. I wonder she has not banged the house down searching for me."

He grinned and tucked her arm into his, and then opened the door and quite efficiently led them both down the hall and into the ballroom together. "Did I not tell you? I caught Mrs. Crabtree as soon as you left and asked her to procure seats, informing her we would join her momentarily. I imagine even now that she is seated, waiting for us. And look! Yes, there she is, with chairs and a little cup of lemonade too. Now, no scowling, my dear, for everyone is looking our way."

CHAPTER EIGHTEEN:

There was one last set forming, and with a wave to a very contented Mrs. Crabtree, Compton maneuvered Lady Lamb through the horde to join at the end. Which is precisely how he received the sharpest pinch under his wrist he had ever known.

He flinched and quickly overturned the minx's hand before she could think to give him another. "You do not have to maul me to get your point across. Now smile. Anyone would think we were having a lovers' spat."

Her eyes glittered dangerously, but she kept a surprisingly affable look upon her face as she gave a little curtsy to begin the number. "You could have stated that Mrs. Crabtree was well and we did not need to come rushing to the ballroom. It is deceitful to play such shams on your partner, as well you know."

"Not if I wish to dance with her. I fear it is merely a delightful way to ensure that I do."

Lady Lamb followed the dance and stepped toward him. He made certain her devilish fingers were well away from the undersides of his wrists as their hands touched, and then twirled her around.

Those enchanting eyes of hers were positively radiant with emotion. He could not look away even if he desired to. She missed a step, and he smoothly dipped with her so no one watching could tell which one of them was at fault. Her face flushed as she broke away from his eyes and focused more on her feet. "No, do not glance at your slippers, my dear. I will not lead you wrongly. However, if you do not keep your gaze on me, they will know, and you will give them fuel for the fire."

"I am not meant to be here. I have not the practice nor the grace to do the quadrille justice."

"Would you prefer to walk about the room? We do not have to finish this dance, if you do not wish it."

She shook her head. "To walk off this floor in the middle of a set? My lord, the scandal! It would give them even more to speak of. Never."

Her foot faltered once again, and he was quick to match her step. Compton could see the rising anxiety upon her features. Truth be told, this was one of the more intricate quadrilles, and not for the faint of heart. With a sharp glance about the room, it was clear to see everyone watching her and judging each stride. How could he have been so blind to have believed they would have watched him when she was clearly ten times the most beautiful woman in the room?

As he dipped once more to cover another misstep, his heart clenched in agony for her. Why were the songs so long? They could not have been dancing but two minutes at most, and they had at least thirteen more of this torture before them. Already he could see the fans fluttering from the women against the walls, hiding their cruel words.

He simply could not keep her here upon this floor enduring such censor. Lending an ear to the beat, he found a delightful six-eight time, which would put them into a medium-paced waltz if he were brave enough to pull her out of the set and begin dancing the outrageous new dance instead.

Her surprise would cover the impropriety on her part nicely, and all eyes and gossip would be once again placed upon his shoulders. No one would expect her to know the steps of the dance, as it was only performed abroad. And the added closeness of the movements would allow him to glide her much more effortlessly. Was he not a scoundrel by the *ton's* rules anyway? But did he dare?

And then Lady Lamb faltered yet again, and he in deep contemplation did not notice until it was too late. The room erupted into smirks and covered giggles.

Without another thought, he dipped and twirled her into his arms. One-two-three. Four-five-six. They spun out of the quadrille and into the center of the room between the four sets of dancers. One-two-three. Four-five-six. The gasps and twitters and quivering fans were filling the area, but it was her large, disbelieving eyes that captured him.

"Lord Compton! Whatever are we doing?"

"We are creating something else for them to talk of, my dear." He moved her around swiftly, and her feet had no choice but to keep up as his arm around her waist became stronger. "Follow me. I promise, no one will blame you for this dance. All fault is now mine."

She stiffened in his arms. However, the one-two-three, four-five-six of the steps became more and more familiar with each stride. It was quite simple to learn the waltz when one kept to the basic paces.

Yet he could see the fear and shame which sought to overtake her in that moment. "Trust me, I beg of you. Ease yourself. I am assisting you as best as I can. Allow me to teach you to soar and enjoy."

Twirling and stepping to her fate, he could tell the indecision was immense—yet he knew the moment she began to compose herself. Her worried eyes met his with frankness, and then a small sliver of pleasure shone through. At that point, she laughed, her voice escalating above all the rest to prove to society that she cared not a fig what any of them whispered.

In that moment, stepping and spinning in her arms, Lord Alistair Compton tumbled completely and utterly in love with Lady Ice, and every soul in the room watched him do so.

CHAPTER NINETEEN:

The rest of the evening was spent in blissful reverie. Compton was reprimanded and several closed fans tapped his arms and shoulders in playful chastisement over his waltz, but he was forgiven. Mainly he was excused because he had brought such a charming lady into the arms of the *ton* again. Several rules of etiquette were exempted because of her that night. He overheard many a lady share the sad story of the heiress losing both of her excellent parents and being shut up in the country until now.

After supper, their hostess allowed Lady Lamb to speak to her husband about Parliament, which bored Lady Stanthorpe close to tears every night and so she welcomed the respite of another person for him to prattle on to. Lord Stanthorpe, having been around a strong wife and daughters, was more than keen to answer the lady's questions about the issues brought up most recently. Compton learned later that he was mighty transfixed with the gel and invited her over any time she wished to learn more.

"You bring her round, and we will be happy to receive you both," Lord Stanthorpe boomed as he approached Compton in a fine drawing room that adjoined the grand hall.

"I certainly will." Compton tilted his head in acknowledgement as the man gestured for him to take a seat on the high-backed chairs clustered together away from the din.

The older lord nodded as they both sat. "Good, good. And if you ever find yourself requiring a seat in Parliament, please allow me to assist you."

Compton's eyes nearly rose to the top of his forehead. "Me? You must be jesting."

"Nay. I have spoken to more than one professor of yours, all with glowing reviews of your diligence in studies and learning. We could use some respectable, resilient young men like you these days. Men who can and do alter the world for the better. Heaven knows, if you are fortunate enough to capture the heart of Lady Lamb, she would continue to inspire and support you through it all. Capital woman! She is remarkable, is she not?"

"You have not known the half of it," Compton agreed. "But I daresay, I fear I will not be the scapegrace who captures her soul. She is much too intelligent to have the wool thrown over her eyes by the likes of me."

Lord Stanthorpe laughed and reached over to pat his shoulder. "Well, my boy, perhaps it is not my place to reprimand you for engaging a lady's name at White's. Nay, I can see by your expression that you are well aware of your portion of idiocy there. Then, perhaps my best counsel to you is to raise your spirits and prove your worth to her. Any fool can see you care for the gel. And despite the imprudence of your very recent past, I believe you to be a superior man than you see yourself to be."

Compton could not fathom how this conversation had turned so awkwardly personal, but instead of balking, a small part of him relished the need for such sound guidance. "Thank you, Lord Stanthorpe. Your words have meant more to me than you comprehend."

He chuckled, his girth bouncing with him. "Aye, my boy, you must remember I was young once as well. At one time, there was the most fine-looking woman in all of London, and I was frantic to make her notice me. I did many a fool thing to win her heart—thankfully, women are much gentler beings than we offer them credit for, and merciful as well. Do they ever need to be merciful! She did at last become aware of me, and notice me regardless of the outlandish effects I attempted to achieve in her favor. My poor beloved Lady Stanthorpe ended up marrying me too. I am a very fortunate man indeed, for I would not be half of what I am without her."

"You are a general, a war hero, and the speaker for the House of Parliament, and you owe these great accomplishments to your wife?" Compton asked with incredulity.

"Yes," the lord replied with a twinkle in his eye as he sat back in his chair. "One day, you will truly understand the worth of the mate of a great man. Without her gentle nudging, extended belief, and constant positive reassurances, I would have given in to my personal fears long before now. However, it is that persistent adoration and support that builds a man. Makes him aspire to be all that she sees in him, and creates the exact person she perceived all along. Women are magical fairies sent to bestow prominence on the men who are clever enough to distinguish the great love they have before them."

In all his years, Compton had never heard such an intriguing statement regarding women in such a way, and yet, he knew what he was hearing was most definitely the truth of the matter. "Well, I am very envious of your state, then. You are fortunate indeed."

"Aye. You will be as well. When she comes around." He nodded his head. "Looks as though the ladies have had the same idea as we, to escape the warm confines of that ballroom."

Compton glanced across the area to the red-headed beauty as she smiled in conversation with a few of the women around Mrs. Crabtree.

Lord Stanthorpe laughed softly. "She is clever, like her father before her. And she is determined. I have never before thought to put a woman in politics, but if there was a woman who could persevere, it is she. Captivating. And not quite the thing at all—but it would seem the rules can be broken a time or two for someone exceptional, eh?"

Compton nodded, no words necessary, for the two lords could not have thought more alike.

"And I daresay she has won her bet. However, perhaps it was not that difficult to be defeated by one like her?" Stanthorpe had turned fully in his seat to observe the ladies they were speaking of.

"I would lose ten times more to have this opportunity."

"When will you concede?"

Compton took a deep breath and positioned himself to fully view Lady Lamb as well. "I do not know. Not yet. I am not quite prepared to see this end."

Lord Stanthorpe nodded and then said, "Well, my lad, you have yourself in a quandary, no doubt, but I would imagine that soon, you shall see the all the good that will come of it. Now, I am off to my study." He groaned a bit as he stood, Compton quick to join him. "Lady Harrington should be satisfied that I managed to stay this long after supper. There are cards in the back room, if you would like to join the older men, though I would think a good share of young ladies would be very put out if you did."

Stanthorpe and Compton began to walk toward the doors nearest the ladies. "I am afraid if I begin to dance with another, my mouse may slip away from the trap."

The older gentleman sighed. "True, true. Well, best of luck to you anyway."

"Thank you, sir. And goodnight." With that, the most interesting conversation Compton had ever had with a peer concluded, and oddly enough, the world seemed to right itself a bit more than it had before.

Mayhap there was still hope to win her hand, though how did one go about doing such a thing without the lady having the least bit of interest in wedding anyone? He continued to stroll over to the door and then leaned up beside the wall not ten feet from Lady Lamb and her chattering gaggle of women.

Lord Hamson sauntered up to him and then rested his shoulder alongside the door casing.

Compton grinned. "Say, when did your wretched carcass arrive?"

Hamson smirked and gave a bit of a shrug. "I have been here longer than you. In fact, I called out to you when you went dashing off after the chit and then concealed yourself in that parlor."

"Devil a bit! You did not."

"No?"

"Pardon me. I honestly had no notion of you being here."

"Or anyone else, for that matter." Hamson nodded in gesture toward the side entrance to the ballroom. Perceval and Atten waved when Compton beheld them.

"Do not tell me." Had they been there all along? To be enamored of a petticoat was one thing, but to be so completely immersed that you do not even recognize your closest companions?

"Aye. All of us have been here, and you have never given any of the lot a by-your-leave or merely said good evening."

Could he have become a bigger nodcock? "I do not know where my mind has gone."

"Do you not?" Hamson glanced over at the pretty lady speaking with Mrs. Crabtree's new friends.

Compton smirked. He feared there was no use hiding anything. "Can you blame me?"

Hamson shifted his stance to face the ballroom and grinned. "Nay, though I do accuse you of attempting to bamboozle us. Anyone but a fool could see that you are in love with the gel. And I am most certainly *not* a fool."

"What am I to do? I cannot deny it—I have no wish to deny it. You are correct. You were not earlier, but I will acknowledge you are most certainly now. However, I have no idea where to go from here."

"Do you think she returns your affections?"

"No. Not in the least. Not yet."

Hamson took a deep breath and then stepped away from the wall, waiting for Compton to follow him. "Then you wait and see what becomes of this all. I believe that within a week, you will know everything you seek."

CHAPTER TWENTY:

Much later that night as Lacey was retiring, Chull came in for a coze and sat upon the chaise lounge in her dressing gown, night cap, and knitted slippers. "You have not said one word about the ball," the old nurse chastised. "If you describe any more expressions Mrs. Crabtree and the others ladies have used about this or that, I will throw my slippers at you. I do not give a fig of what they have had to speak of tonight, only what your thoughts are."

Lacey laughed. "Good heavens. I have not seen you this out of sorts since I was a little girl." She sat down at her dressing table and allowed her abigail to start pulling out her hairpins. "Thank you, Annie. You made me look like a princess tonight. Many people commented on my hair."

The girl of sixteen blushed. "Thank you, my lady. I am happy to see you were so well received. And I, too, am anxious to hear of all that happened with Lord Compton."

"You as well?" Lacey shook her head. "Between the two of you, I will get no rest until I reveal all."

"Serves you right," Chull said. "You are merely giving us the fluff and fat and nothing of the good meat."

"Good meat? What cant!" Lacey began to brush at the long locks that were coming undone as the abigail removed each pin. "Very well, I shall tell you that I only danced once all night. Is that what you wish to hear? Who my dancing partners were?"

Chull folded her arms. "You know very well that is precisely what I wish to know. I have no doubt, then, that it was Lord Compton. And what happened? Why did you only dance once? And do not attempt to say no one else would have you, because I shall not believe it."

"Nay, plenty of gentlemen attempted to ask after we were through, but as it was clear I had no notion of what I was doing, I remained frank and honest in my responses to them."

"Yes." Chull fluttered her hands. "But tell me of Compton. Surely he was forgiving of your lack of knowledge of the steps?"

Lacey paused and thought back to him, then replied more seriously. "Honestly, if it were not for him, I would have returned home immediately I came."

"No! What happened?" asked Annie.

"I walked into the ballroom, and as soon as those nearest learned my name, it spread and the chin-wagging began, and I could not stay another moment. But then Lord Compton caught me up and talked me through it all, and before I knew what he was about, I was joining him on the floor for the King's Quadrille."

Chull gasped. "Oh, dear! That one is exceptionally difficult."

The brush faltered in Lacey's hand. "As both Lord Compton and I soon acknowledged. I simply could not keep up with the steps."

"How mortifying." Annie's hands paused.

"Yes, the room was in stitches, all the fine ladies laughing at my expense."

"Did you stride off the floor? I do not think I could have stayed on," the abigail asked.

"Nay, I would have, but I was afraid the gabblemongers would become worse for my doing so."

"No doubt you are right. Carry on," Chull pressed her. "Did you just muddle through as best you could?"

Lacey began to brush at her hair again, her heart growing slightly warmer than it had been moments before. "Nay, Lord Compton surprised me and whirled me away from our set and into the middle of the ballroom, where we began to waltz."

"Waltz?" Chull clutched her dressing gown to her neck and whispered, "Certainly he did not dare do such a thing. What did the others say? What did they do?"

"Blather on, of course." She smiled at the memory. "I was at first terrified, scandalized, shocked—I had no notion of what to do except follow him. However, he was persistent and spoke to me of what he was doing and why—and then I comprehended what he was truly achieving." She bit her lip and stared at her reflection in the looking glass, even then contemplating Lord Compton's magnanimous gesture. "His sole purpose was to rescue me."

Through the reflection, Lacey saw the horror on the older woman's face slowly slip into awe and then gratitude. "You are correct, my dear. That is exactly what he did."

"All at once, I felt such an overabundance of joy come upon me, I could not help myself—I laughed. Spinning around in the arms of the handsome rogue, I giggled like a girl who had just won the May Queen, finally freeing myself of the worries and thoughts of anyone else."

The housekeeper nodded. "Although it was most brazen of you, I am grateful to hear you enjoyed yourself."

Lacey turned in her seat, causing Annie to step back. "That is not all! After supper, I spoke with Lord Stanthorpe, the Speaker of the House, for nearly a half an hour about Parliament, making tonight by far the most enjoyable evening I have ever had."

"It sounds just so." The older woman sat up on the lounge.

"If it were not for Lord Compton's insistence, I never would have gone."

"And have you thanked the young lord?" The old nurse was forever reminding her of her manners.

Lacey turned back toward the mirror and frowned. "No, I admit it completely slipped my mind. Now whatever should I do? How does one go about thanking a gentleman?"

"Well …" Chull grinned. "One could perhaps agree to spend the day with him when he asks next."

Lacey flushed. "I supposed I could do something as simple as that."

"Do you wish to do more?" Annie asked quietly.

She shook her head. "No, definitely not. Still, I am never happy until I have repaid my debts." Lacey's gaze met Chull's through the looking glass.

Chull let out a soft groan as she climbed out of the chaise lounge. "I am certain you will think of just the thing, my dear. Given time, you will know how to make it all right."

As the last of the pins came out of her hair, Lacey turned in her seat once more. "Chull, how will …" She trailed off, not sure what she was trying to say.

"Yes?"

Lacey gave her head a little shake. "'Twas nothing. Merely thinking out loud, I guess."

Chull paused, her hand upon the doorknob, and gave a warm grin. "My dearest, you will never fully apprehend what your mind is pondering until you finally permit your heart to speak."

Lacey blinked, not entirely certain she was ready to understand that thought.

Thankfully, Chull did not press the issue. "Goodnight, my dear. I am very pleased you enjoyed yourself."

CHAPTER TWENTY-ONE:

The next morning, a full bouquet of irises made their way into a certain home on Green Street, and the whole house was in a tizzy over it. Everyone knew that with such a bouquet of irises, there must be a message of some importance attached. Indeed, there was a letter tied neatly to the wrapped bouquet, but Lady Lamb was still asleep in her bed. Pantersby handed the flowers over to Chull, who found a vase and arranged them sweetly upon the table in the green drawing room, all the while sharing with him exactly what their sweet Lady Lamb had revealed the night before.

"Are you certain she laughed when Lord Compton swirled her out for the waltz?"

"Aye. She even admitted that he rescued her."

Pantersby was having the devil of a time hiding his grin, so chuffed was he that Lady Lamb was finally beginning to heal. "Just like a knight upon a white charger coming to her aid."

[121]

Chull and Pantersby walked into the kitchen and then over to the small room with a table to the side. "Do you perchance believe this could lead to something?" Chull asked as Cook brought in a tray of tea.

Cook herself smiled at the thought. "Oh, I very much hope so! He is so handsome."

Pantersby gave a slight frown at the woman, who curtsied and then scurried away. "He seems a good man. I pray he is, for her sake."

Chull handed over a cup and saucer. "She would not have fallen in love with him else."

He nearly choked on his tea. "Do you think she has by now lost her heart?"

She took a sip and sighed. "It would be wonderful if she did. Oh, Pantersby! Do not look at me like that. You know how much she has despised this world and lived in such mad mistrust. And whatever for? Because she does not feel she is worthy of them."

"Well, that is a very foolish thought, for there is no greater lady in all of society."

"I know—I know this well. Now, if only we can make her see herself as so."

Pantersby huffed as he took another sip. "I only wish I knew what that letter contained. I vow I will call the man out if he intends to harm her."

She giggled. "You cannot call him out, as well you know, so stop your drivel. And I do not think he means to harm her." Chull leaned forward and got a glimpse of Cook wiping down the doorway nearest them with a cloth, intently listening in. "Do you know at what cost he led her away from the dreadful quadrille out into the waltz? Any pride he had left would have been in shreds. Why, everyone turned their attention to him and immediately forgave her.

So much so that she was then able to spend half an hour talking to Lord Stanthorpe about Parliament."

"You do not say." Pantersby's mouth dropped open. "I am in astonishment."

"Aye, so was I. But it would seem she has been finally accepted by the *ton* and enjoyed herself immensely."

When the servants' bell rang, they both jumped and then looked at each other.

"She is awake!" Chull set her cup down first, straightened her dress, and nearly beat Annie to Lady Lamb's door.

It took another twenty minutes or so, but finally the lady was walking down the stairs and into the green drawing room to see what all the fuss was about.

Lacey was pleasantly surprised at the number of irises in the vase. "Did he buy out all of London just for me?" Her hand shook as she took the card and walked over to the high-backed chair to open it. It was not dreadfully long, but certainly long enough to appease the strictest of critiques of gentlemen's letters. She was also pleased to note that it was written in an elegant hand.

Lady Lamb,

I thank you for the privilege of standing up with me for the first set, and for the sweetness with which you accepted my reprehensible ways in insisting we dance the waltz. You were a very gracious and charming partner whose beauty outshone every other lady there. It is with my deepest respect that I send you this bouquet, and I hope you accept the irises.

These flowers are a particular favorite of mine. Beautiful, elegant, and they are accompanied with an air of hopeful things to come.

I did not have the chance to relay a bit of what Lord Stanthorpe divulged to me after you and he had parted. Allow me to do so now. He was exceptionally taken with you and found you both bright and clever. It was my honor to hear him expound upon your lively mind with a keen interest, and that lord even went as far as revealing that if a woman were to be in politics, he would certainly believe it could be you.

It is my greatest pleasure to have been acquainted with you, and I hope we may continue to be great friends, confiding and growing together. I feel you have much to teach me, and I would gladly be your pupil and learn all that I can at your feet. If you are willing, I will be by at half past one to call upon you. Until then,

> *Your humble servant, etc. etc.*
> *Alistair Compton*

Half past one? Lacey glanced up at the clock and then breathed a sigh of relief. She knew she had been a slug-a-bed and slept the morning through, but it was merely noon, so all was not as lost as it seemed. There was nothing more than a simple greeting in his letter. Certainly not as much as the excitement that was created to guarantee she opened the thing. She smiled and then looked up at the hopeful faces of Chull and Pantersby. "Would you like to read it?" she asked as she held the missive out for them.

Neither moved. "Come now, you cannot fool me." She set the letter down upon the table nearest. "There. I will leave it and go to the breakfast room, and you two can read it to your hearts' content."

Chull moved first. "Does he reveal anything at all?" she asked as she snatched it up.

"No. As you will soon see." Lacey made her way into the breakfast room, and Cook was quick to send out a maid with a few small platters of meat, fruit, and bread.

A couple of seconds later, in skipped in little Mary and Emma, Cook's girls. Each of them brought silverware and plates, with embroidered napkins too. "Good day, La'ly Lamb!" Mary beamed, her dark braids bopping as she curtsied.

"La'ly Lamb, we brought your plates so's you can eat." Emma dipped into a curtsy as well. Her pinafore was held out with one hand, charmingly imitating a grand lady.

"Thank you." Lacey grinned as she collected their offerings. She was certain there were not two more endearing children anywhere.

"We gots to go, La'ly Lamb," Emma said. "We're Mama's helpers ta-day."

She chuckled. "Very well. Run along then, imps."

"Your flowers are beautiful, my lady," Cook said as she appeared moments later with the tea.

"Yes, though why you are all in tremblings over the things, I cannot imagine." Lacey's heart stopped for a moment over the lie.

"Aye, but it is the first time you have ever received flowers from a gentleman, my lady."

"You are meaning besides a simple posy?"

"Yes." Cook's eyes sparkled with excitement.

Lacey could not understand her own household. Why were they so eager? "Have you seen Lord Compton?" she asked, surprised at the reaction his flowers brought.

"Oh, yes. When he came to see the puppies."

Of course. Lacey had almost forgotten the little tykes. "And did he speak with you?"

"Yes, he was very polite and kind to me and the girls."

Suddenly, Lacey could not breathe. Her foolish heart could not fathom what she was hearing. After a few moments, once the beating slowed a bit, she asked, "Lord Compton has spoken with the girls as well?"

"Aye, my lady. He played with them on the floor. The girls love him so."

For no apparent reason, tears flooded her eyes, and she quickly dashed them away. Could it be possible? Could that horrendously wonderful beast be kind enough to take time out of his day to see the servants too? Nay, not only see them, but take a moment to talk with them and play with them? Was it possible he was not as arrogant as the rest of his breed?

One could forgive a man a great deal if he was willing to prove his kind heart. She would wager a hundred pounds there was no other lord in London who would do half as much. Her own brother was not one to tolerate servants, and he knew her desires and beliefs more than Lord Compton ever had. And yet, her brother still created moments of disdain and indifference toward those she would call family.

Apart from placing the bet for her to protect the family name, and the odd country parties he and his wife partook of that Lacey sometimes attended, she and her brother really did move in completely different circles. They could and did speak of politics, but Melbourne and his wife were more set in their ways and not as appreciative of her interest in government as Lord Stanthorpe had been. It was because of their slight condescension that Lacey had purchased this home to begin with. It had become very clear that they did not wish her to stay with them during the Parliament season yet another year now that she could afford a home of her own.

Lacey stared out the window and blindly marveled at the servants' delight over Lord Compton's attention. She was a bluestocking, and not at all the fashionable sort. Her dancing was appalling, her manners unguarded and uncouth, and she was constantly judging those he would call friends. She could not fathom the man being the least bit interested in her.

The hardest lesson for her to grasp last evening was that society, while unbearably gossipy, was not as wholly bad as she imagined them to be. Indeed, Lacey enjoyed herself much more than she could have ever hoped.

"My lady!" Pantersby rushed in, all flustered fervor. In fact, she had never seen him so ruffled before. "This letter is signed simply Alistair Compton."

"Yes?"

"He signed his Christian name. No title—merely Alistair Compton. My dear, the man is utterly in love with you."

CHAPTER TWENTY-TWO:

For the first time, Lacey found herself in a completely new state of mind. These nerves that accompanied every single thought were much more vexing than any she had known before. Indeed, they were much worse than when she attended the ball last night, more than when her anger at meeting Lord Compton belied every bit of dignity she had as she restrained herself from quartering the sop. Yet, this—this was an unnatural, surreal experience. Every single thing suddenly mattered. Her hair, her petticoat, her necklace, her gown—even her shoes were brought into question at least eight times as she tried them on over and over again.

If she had thought her hands shook before, it was nothing to the ridiculousness she was forced to bear at this moment. Furthermore, even her teacup could not be picked up without sloshing the hot liquid everywhere. She was a disgraceful wreck!

Her stomach fluttered and churned—honestly, if she was not so eager to see Lord Compton once more, she would have convinced herself she had fallen very ill. Preposterous! Ludicrous! Incompressible anxiety! By the time one o'clock rolled around, she was positive she would never be herself again.

And then he came!

Her foolish heart beat frantically in response, and she knew not where to look until he walked up and kissed the top of each hand and then grinned that devastatingly handsome grin at her. "Hello there, Lady Lamb. How is your day?"

And then for no particular reason, she wanted to wipe that complacent grin off his face and kiss those dastardly lips, which could be why she answered him a mite more frustrated than she had intended. "All was well until your flowers and letter arrived."

"Do you not like irises?" he asked, confusion marring his features.

Lacey's gaze met his. She felt her nerves growing, yet could not be unkind. "Yes. They are beautiful. Forgive me, Lord Compton, I—"

"Please call me Alistair. Are we not friends enough for that?"

All other thoughts fled her mind and her mouth opened up, but she could not speak. For truly, her heart had never beat so rapidly before.

"I see I have shocked you. Excuse me." He glanced away, his eyes finding the bouquet. "I fear I may have been a bit too earnest this morning. If you would like me to leave, I will do so at once."

She must say something to him. "L—Lord Compton, please, do not. We have come off to a bad start. Let us begin anew." She held her hand out for him to shake. "Hello, my lord."

He gave a rueful grin and took her hand, shaking it shortly and then kissing the back yet again.

Lacey flushed and then took a deep breath. She was never good at receiving men, and even more so now that she had been so out of practice. However, if she could but find her courage, perhaps she would not injure him more. "I would like us to be friends."

Compton's gaze searched hers. "Indeed?"

Her smile wavered as her heart beat so loudly, she was certain he must hear it too. "Yes, please."

"And as friends, am I impertinent to ask you to call me Alistair?"

Could it really mean that he was in love with her? Was Pantersby correct? "No. Though, to be fair, you must call me Lacey."

Alistair smiled and let out a sigh. "I would be most pleased to, Lacey."

Every centimeter of her was filled to the brim with a tingly sensation she had never experienced before. Now what was to be done? It was all of a sudden awkward, and too quiet by half.

Compton must have seen her distress. "Would you like to chat awhile, or may I take you elsewhere? Perhaps to explore Hyde Park or Grosvenor Square, if you wish?"

Oh! Of course. Where were her manners? "Please, have a seat. I will ring for tea."

He chuckled. "Lady Lamb, er, Lacey, unless you are famished, let us go somewhere. It is a lovely day, and I think a bit of a walk would do us both good. Also, as you can see, I came an hour earlier than is fashionable. I fear if we stay in the home a minute longer, several gentlemen will be clamoring at your door."

[130]

"Mine?" Was he mad? "Whatever for?"

"Because, my dear, those who were at the Stanthorpes' last night could not but help getting a glimpse of you. I had hoped to make it before the throng."

"You have lost your mind, Lord Compton—Alistair— if you believe that any young pup will come knocking about my door. Not only am I much too old to be considered marriageable, but I have yet to truly speak to any of them."

As if on cue to some ridiculous farce, Pantersby arrived with a missive.

"My lady, this was brought to the door just now. A servant of a young gentleman—Lord Althorpe—wishes to take you round Hyde Park at four. His man is awaiting your response."

Compton had the audacity to laugh, though he was kind enough to walk to the other side of the room while she responded. "Good heavens. Tell him thank you, but I am previously engaged."

Pantersby glanced at the tall man in the corner and then winked at Lacey. "Very good, my lady."

As he left, Compton turned round and asked again, "Shall we?"

She grinned at that knowing face and answered simply, "I shall fetch my bonnet directly."

CHAPTER TWENTY-THREE:

It was a very rare spring day with the sun shining so brightly. Wrapped head to toe in delightful green flounces and embroidered white dots, Lady Lacey Lamb could not have looked prettier, and the matching parasol and bonnet only added to her adorable figure. Her arm was wrapped snugly through the handsome Lord Alistair Compton's, and many a head turned back to see them smiling and engaged in witty conversation so early in the afternoon.

Gabblemongers who were at present with the latest gossip stopped in wonder as the two passed by, nodding and smiling as if they did not have a care in the world.

However, that was far from the case. Indeed, Lord Compton was at that precise moment, as they walked aimlessly toward Grosvenor Square, eagerly sharing with his attentive partner Lord Stanthorpe's words of him joining Parliament.

"And what are your thoughts about this?" Lacey asked as her hand clung tighter to the sleeve of his coat. "Is government something that interests truly you?"

Compton glanced down at those hopeful eyes and felt his chest swell with the thought that this dear lady might come around. "Indeed, it was at one time. It held the chief of my thoughts for several years of my youth."

"And now?" she asked.

"I do not know. It has been so long since I have pushed that part of my life away, I have not gone back until recently. Very recently. Or rather, I was pacing my rooms until six this morning pondering on the realities of such an adventure."

"May I ask which side you supported once upon a time?"

He looked away and grinned bashfully. "I am afraid to say it was . . . I presume the exact opposite of your desires."

"No!" She gasped and laughed, causing several more heads to speculate on them both as they passed by a large shop. "You are a Tory!"

"I *was* a Tory. I am nothing at the moment. Some days, I do not know where to turn my head. However, I do not understand how you could be as wealthy as you are, and a viscountess, and yet, be a Whig."

Lady Lamb shook her head in amazement. "If I can use my fortuitous opportunities to help others, I will always do so. My rank does not matter as a daily issue is concerned, though if it can be an example to another, I am glad for it." She halted and turned toward him. "You cannot possibly believe in the slave trade, as others do."

"I did at one time, but I have since grown and seen the humanity that my father tried to snuff out from me. It is one of the reasons why it was so easy for me to leave the idea of politics behind."

"Do you not realize the good the Whig party is attempting to bring to the people of England? Why, even now children's labor is being investigated, and they are currently writing up laws that will allow the government to help the poor and uneducated." She shook her head in disgust. "The Tories have only ever thought of themselves. Afraid to advance forward and allow the people to govern the kingdom. It will always be a hierarchy in their minds, and they do much to attempt to keep it that way."

"Your passion does you credit. I have learned more from you during this short time we have been acquainted than I have ever learned in my life."

"I do not wish to force anyone into beliefs of mine. I would much rather you searched within yourself and found a suitable fit."

"I am not so easily swayed as to jump into the opinions of the first lovely lady I meet. However, you are wholly good. With such a supreme example of charity that you naturally exude, I cannot deny that your presence and thoughts are utterly life-changing. Last night as I was contemplating this rather unexpected shift in my existence, I came to the conclusion that if all men and women had your desires, England would be exceptionally strong and just."

She blushed and looked away. "You flatter me, my lord."

"It is more than flattery, I assure you. It is how I truly feel whenever our paths cross and I am once again uplifted by your faith and kindness."

"I am not the only soul with such thoughts and actions. My servants tell me you have spent time speaking with them. Does that not prove that you are above reproach as well?"

"Hardly!" he snorted. "Nay, do not over-romanticize my actions into painting me anything other than black. Have you forgotten that I am the man tactless enough to place your name in the betting books at White's?"

She paused in front of a shop window and stared fully at him. "I have not forgotten, but I am quickly forgiving that action."

His heart began to thump strangely. "Lady Lamb, are you in jest?"

"Sir! You would make it seem as if you did not believe a word that came out of my mouth. Yes, I am pardoning you. You are not fully absolved, but it will come soon, I am sure."

"You have made me a very happy man." When she blushed once again, he changed the subject. "So, we have seven more events to attend. Are you looking forward to tomorrow at the Vauxhall Gardens?"

"I have never been, but I have heard they are diverting. One of my brother's friends mentioned that they have a fireworks display every night."

"'Tis true."

"Now that I long to see." She took a deep breath and stepped forward, Compton quick to join. "Will your friends like me overly much?" she asked.

Compton realized she must know full well they would be attending Vauxhall with the very men who were present when he placed his bet. "Lord Hamson, Lord Atten, and Lord Perceval are amongst your foremost supporters. They have—all of them—removed their money from mine and placed theirs on your counter bet. They also spend a good deal of time pressing me into admitting I am in love with you."

"They do?" Her eyes were wide, and her mouth sweetly opened.

In fact, if they were not walking down the street this very moment, he would have swept her in his arms and kissed those lips. Compton cleared his throat. "Yes, which I deny as best I can. It is getting much more difficult, though." He glanced her way and then back out into the street. Grasp what she would make of that admission.

"It is?"

He could see her darling smile peek out the corners of her mouth, but when she ducked her head, the pesky bonnet hid her face too much. He decided that was enough gentle prodding for the day. There was much for her to contemplate—from the seat in Parliament, to the Vauxhall Gardens, and then the admission of reply to his companions. For the rest of their time together, he completely kept all heavier subjects off limits and allowed the two of them to enjoy each other's company so that by early evening when he went into her kitchens and said goodnight to the puppies, there was nothing but blissful conversation and perhaps—with a bit of luck—a moment or two when the gel wondered how she had ever gotten on without him there.

Compton whistled as he took his hat from Pantersby and skipped down the steps of her home. Today he had decided to walk. He needed something to clear his head from his frantic heart. Perhaps he was interpreting it all wrong. Perhaps he was not winning her at all, but whatever transpired, he found it was worth the risk, for he truly was never jollier than he was with her.

As he strolled past White's, Compton took a few steps backward, and then without ceremony, entered the gentlemen's club. Very calmly, he strode to the betting counter and asked to have his name and bet removed. He paid the fine and relinquished the rest of the money to be sent back to those who had bid for him. Then he very cheekily wrote in large letters, placing another bout of his own money upon Lady Lamb's bet, announcing to the *ton* that she had most perfectly and fairly won.

CHAPTER TWENTY-FOUR:

The very next day, Compton sent a letter round to Lord Stanthorpe, requesting to speak to him about a seat in Parliament. After a fretful morning of deliberating if the man had only said such things to him to be kind, he received his answer—to meet at his office in the Palace of Westminster that very day at three.

"My lord, I have never seen you in such high fidgets as this," Terrell chastised as he placed Compton's best day suit upon his shoulders. "You act as though your very life depends upon this meeting."

"It does, Terrell. My whole very existence rests on what will happen within the next hour or so."

"Well, it is no wonder, for you have ruined three cravats with all of your apprehension. I will now need to wash and starch them all over again."

The last thing Compton wanted to discuss was his neck cloths. He reached over, grabbed the man's arm, and took a deep breath. "Tell me I am not a fool."

Terrell paused a moment and clutched Compton's other arm. "You are not a fool. You are a man who is recalling who he once was. And, my lord, may I say how proud of you we all are? The staff and I have been very excited to see such changes in you."

"Truly?"

"Yes. You have always been a good man, and now you have an opportunity to demonstrate it."

He shook his head. "No, Terrell, I have been a wastrel of a man who buried my head in the sand and cared not for anything but myself for far too long."

"You were a man in mourning."

"Allow me to own what I was. If it was mourning, I was indolent enough to enjoy the frivolities of the essence of woe and not what I should have been doing—living life. Nay, I have been hiding, and I am extremely grateful to have finally woken up, so to speak."

"Do you feel that way, as though you have become awake after a long slumber?"

"Yes. Precisely that. And it is a marvelous feeling."

Lord Stanthorpe was true to his promise, and the discussion went as well as Compton could have hoped. The workplace had its own set of doors that allowed for privacy. The room resembled that of a large study one would find in a stately manor in the country. It was lined with ancient books on shelves that looked to be hundreds of years old, with patriotic artwork from around Europe and England.

They did not have an opening for him in the House of Lords just yet, but Stanthorpe was keen on placing him there within the year, especially after speaking with him and hearing his newly founded Whig tendencies.

"There are other lords who speak for the Whigs, but I would like to see more, as there have been a few Tories recently who have been openly berating the changes happening in England. They want life returned as it was ages ago, but it will never be that way again. It cannot go back or I fear England will fall. This new direction is giving our nation her morals once again, and increasing awareness in other countries as well."

"Others? Do you mean the other colonies we own?"

"No, I am speaking of the Americas, who rightfully thrust England out."

"I do not fully understand your meaning. What are the Americans to do with the Whigs?"

"They looked to the Whigs as heroes, and at one point, before becoming patriots, called themselves such."

"Fascinating."

"My hands are tied as the Speaker. I am the middle ground, but mark my words, if England is to abolish slavery, the Americans will follow suit, and can you imagine the joys that will come of such a thing? The lives those people can finally reclaim and press forward with a future and hope for themselves?"

Compton felt a little overwhelmed. "You speak as Lady Lamb does."

He leaned back in his chair. "Well, as you leave, I will hand over a list of newspapers, books, and pamphlets to catch you back up to snuff with the rest of the world." He leaned over and patted Compton's shoulder. "And share them with your Lady Lamb. I am curious to hear what her words would be on such subjects."

"I most certainly will."

"Remember, Lord Compton, I would ask you to attend our meetings as an observer most diligently. I would that you came often and studied our ways. I have hopes to present you to the House of Lords before the season is up as we retire a few of our seats this year. Some of our members have become much too old, and this is the perfect year for you become a part of this great government.

"Hopefully, by next year, you will be grafted in without issue. Look about you. See where change is needed, and watch how these ideas and others are being presented to Parliament so you are prepared to bring up your own causes. Though there are a few appointed seats, I fear yours will need to be voted in. I implore you to be present, be active, and introduce yourself and speak to as many of the lords as you can."

Compton nodded, his chest already becoming much lighter at the prospect of being able to assist others. All at once, it was as if he had a voice again, as if his life mattered, and he was of a greater purpose than he could imagine. "Thank you so very much for giving me this opportunity. I feel as though the dreams of my youth are coming back once more."

Stanthorpe smiled. "It is a marvelous ability to do what one has always wished to do rather than what one has been told he must do. In your case, you are a very fortunate man indeed. I trust that you will succeed and go farther than you can expect at this moment."

"Your support means the world to me."

"Nay, I am only opening a door. The support of your wife will be what propels you forward. You do plan to wed her, do you not?"

"Will you tease me about Lady Lamb each time we speak?"

"Quite possibly, though perhaps if you were to marry, I would not feel so inclined to do so."

So caught up in reading what Lord Stanthorpe had sent home with him, Compton just about forgot the time and would have missed Vauxhall Gardens with Lady Lamb if it were not for his butler.

"My lord, were you not planning an evening out?" Johnson asked as he knocked upon the study door.

Compton dropped the pamphlet on his desk and jumped up. "Yes! Thank you," he said as he rushed out of the study. "Terrell!" he shouted down the house. "Terrell! I need my blue coat—quickly!"

The ever-faithful Terrell had his clothes previously laid out. "You are a god!" Compton grinned as he swiftly began to change.

"Well, I have always known my worth, my lord. It is nice to see that you have finally recognized it as well."

"Cheeky." He laughed as a new white shirt was slipped over his broad shoulders. "Thank you. There are times when I would not be alive if it were not for you."

"Undoubtedly." Terrell sniffed as he began to button up the waistcoat.

CHAPTER TWENTY-FIVE:

The Vauxhall Gardens were unbelievably beautiful, and Lacey could not fathom how it was that she had been in London in the past and yet had never seen them. There was a stage with performers, and little paths that took one on whimsical adventures and the like. The whole of the grounds were an endless possibility of entertainment and wonder. If she had spent three nights there, she doubted she would have seen everything the park had to offer.

With its many people and sometimes crowded paths, it was nice to sit down and have a small respite of tea and scones at the tea shop in the park grounds. Lord Compton's friends were agreeable, and the young ladies who accompanied them were affable as well, but it was Lady Perceval Lacey enjoyed most.

"Are you enjoying yourself?" that lady asked as she sipped her tea.

"Oh, so very much! I had not an inkling this place would be so dreamlike. I wonder at how much time it took to build the little huts and decorations along the paths."

"I do not know, but it has been here forever, and entertained several people for years."

"It must have been a modern marvel, I am sure."

"It is a modern marvel still!" Lady Perceval chortled. "Wait until you see the fireworks. Then you shall truly be amazed."

"Oh, I hope so."

Lord Compton leaned appallingly across her plate and snitched a bit of jam that had fallen. And then asked matter-of-factly, as if he had done no such thing, "There is still half hour or so before the fireworks commence. Could I tempt you to take a turn around the gardens for a few of those minutes?"

Lacey took the last sip of her tea and then answered, "Of course. Please excuse me, Lady Perceval. It appears this scamp would like to take me away."

She laughed. "Not at all—there is no excuse needed. Enjoy yourself. I promise, he improves the longer you know him."

Lacey smiled. "Well then, that may be a relief."

"I can hear you both perfectly well," he said as he took her hand into his. Compton maneuvered them away from the table and the prying eyes of all present.

"You do not need to be quite so forward, my lord," she said as he placed her hand in the crook of his elbow. "You need only ask for the jam, and I would have handed over the plate."

"Do I not? I find the greatest way to get a lady's attention is to do something so outrageous, she immediately stops talking. I thought you would never stop your prattling with the woman. I adore Georgianna

Perceval as much as the next man, but when I have eagerly awaited a moment alone with you all evening, you must understand my keenness at taking whatever opportunities present themselves. Or, creating my own when they do not become readily available."

She chuckled. "You are a monster."

"Indeed, I am. A selfish one too, for I do not wish to share you with anyone."

"Shameful!"

They skirted past several people, winding around the bend, until Compton pulled them off onto a much more secluded path that made its way around the far corner of the park. It was fairly lit, but with no marked opening, only a tight gap between two hedges.

"How did you know this was here?" she asked.

"I have my ways." He looked down at her, smugly grinning, his hat tilted to a jaunty angle. They wandered a few more meters down the cobbled path before coming to a quaint stone bench. Then he startled her by asking, "May I speak earnestly to you, Lacey?"

Without warning, her heart rate began to triple in pace. Whatever could he be about? "Yes, I suppose so," she said as composedly as possible.

Compton sat down upon the bench and gently placed her right next to him, the flounces of her pale pink gown fanning out charmingly around her. "I have some news to impart," he said.

Unexpectedly, she decided to explain, at least partially, how she had grown fond of him. "I do as well," she replied after taking a breath to calm her nerves. Apparently, it would seem that quiet paths in the gardens beneath starry nights is where deep secrets are revealed.

He looked intrigued. "And what have you to share? Nothing bad, I hope."

She gave a shaken smile, flummoxed about how to answer such a thing. "I do not know if good or ill will come of parting with what I have to tell you. However, I believe—or rather hope—that good things will come to pass."

Those dark eyes of his examined her features as she desperately attempted to gain the pluck she needed to speak.

"Will you leave me in suspense?" he asked with a hint of a smile.

"I find myself unexpectedly nervous to speak now. Embarrassed, even."

Compton took one of her small hands in his. "Do not be, sweetling."

Sweetling? Lacey wondered at how she could be so brazen in this moment. Yet, with his declarations earlier, it would be horrid if she did not express something of what she felt. "I have grown to admire you, Lord—Alistair. When I spoke with my servants again, long after we returned from seeing Grosvenor Square, they said once more how you were kind to Cook and her girls as you played with the puppies."

He shifted on the bench a bit. "I do not understand. It was nothing."

"Chull, my housekeeper, said you sent each of the little girls a posy this morning, though I did not hear of it until after you had gone." Her heart swelled at the memory of the joy and pride on the little girls' faces when they showed her. "You completely won them over and made their day so very special. Thank you for being kind to them."

"I honestly would have forgotten I gave them flowers at all, had you not mentioned it."

"You are too modest. Even if you did not think of it, I am certain they thought of little else today, and will undoubtedly talk about that small gesture for years to come."

"Surely not."

She chuckled and clasped his other hand. "Do not underestimate the love a female has for flowers from a lord."

"Do you speak from experience?" He grinned and brought his head in very close to hers.

Her breath froze as her gaze flitted over his handsome features. "Oh, most definitely."

"Was that what you wished to tell me?" he whispered. "To share that little tykes will talk about me sending them flowers for the rest of their lives? Was this what truly had you so nervous?"

"No." She pulled away from him and grinned. "Cease mocking me. I wish you to know that I am enormously honored to call you friend. You are unbelievably thoughtful and gentle, and I am so very lucky to have you close to me." She took a deep breath. "Although I was cross and said unforgivable things to you, I am so grateful for every experience you have had, for without them, I would not see this cherished friend before me. Each and every past experience, or difficulty, or scandalous thing has only grown to produce the kindness that you are. Thank you for allowing me to see the goodness around me—that bit of life I had denied myself because of my own prejudices."

She squeezed his fingers. "Alistair, yet again you have proven that there is worth in everything."

He leaned forward and kissed her gently on the lips, and in that unexpected moment, Lacey's heart burst.

"Forgive me." He pulled back and caught her gaze. "However, I do not feel the least bit remorseful."

Lacey returned his mischievous smile. "Nor I."

She watched, fascinated, as Compton closed his eyes and took a deep breath. "I cannot begin to hope like this. You will surely destroy me if I do. Please do not trifle with me, Lady Lamb. If you do not feel a thing for me, let it be revealed now, for I fear I am slipping."

Was he truly in love with her? Was this how a gentleman acted when he was anxious? Lacey leaned forward and kissed him again, relishing his soft lips upon hers, her boldness causing her to blush. "I have no intention of destroying anyone, least of all you, Alistair."

"How?" His earnest looks nearly unsettled her. "How are you such an angel to forgive me so?"

"And I am to wonder how you are such a man to show affection for me despite my prudence and outspoken passions and stiff nature. I am by far the least accomplished woman of your acquaintance, and yet you look over it all to appreciate me."

"What is this gibberish?" He looked astonished as he pulled away. "Not accomplished? Lady Lamb, I will never hear of you speak of such a thing again. I feel like a simpleton in your presence. You are so much more exceptional than I will ever be."

Lacey stared at the perplexing man a full minute before asking, "Do you honestly see me in such a light?"

"Yes!" he blurted.

She could not help but laugh. "What a wretched pair we make!"

He gasped at her admission, though it took a half beat more for her to ascertain what had been admitted out loud.

Compton held up a hand. "No, do not speak another word. I wish to remember this night precisely as it is right at this moment."

"Why is that?"

"Because I fear that you may break this spell. It must be an enchantment you are under to be uttering such nonsense, and very shortly, you shall come to your senses and run like mad away from me and all that I am."

She wanted to curl herself up in his embrace, to kiss him again a thousand times, to embrace him and never let go, yet propriety held her fast to her seat. However, one wayward hand reached up and touched that very dear cheek. "You are a scoundrel, but I am very much afraid to say you will forever be my scoundrel soon."

Compton turned his jaw into her hand and kissed the palm. It was a chaste, simple kiss—but full of more love, devotion, and promise that she had ever acknowledged before.

Could it all be possible? Could she finally, truly be in love?

CHAPTER TWENTY-SIX:

Quietly, Alistair stood and pulled Lacey up. He enfolded her into his arms, gently embracing her for a few moments before drawing her hand into the crook of his elbow once more. He simply could not help staring at her. Those bewitching eyes, the glowing hair, the warm smile. All of this person before him was beyond anything he could have ever imagined.

He had almost spoken to her of his meeting with Lord Stanthorpe earlier. However, he was grateful now that he had not. What if he did not get the position after all? No, it was better to wait, yet he gathered that by going back into government, he would not have the time with her he had been enjoying of late. His heart saddened a little at the thought. "Lacey?"

"Yes?"

"I must beg your pardon, but I find I will not be able to attend the Dodderings' afternoon gala Wednesday next.

In fact, I am afraid I will not be seeing much of you at all during the day. I am now needed elsewhere."

He could tell she was curious, but she was good enough not to pry. "Should I go to the gala alone, then?" Her face fell. "No. Perhaps I should cry off as well. Furthermore, I have vowed only to attend the events where I know I will not make a mockery of myself."

"You will never be seen in such a light, I promise you."

"Perhaps not by you, but as for a good many others, I most certainly shall." She took a few more unhurried steps and then added, "By and by, it does not wholly matter, for I doubt I will attend another ball again."

"Unless I am there to sweep you into a scandalous waltz?"

She laughed. "You are incorrigible. I meant, as long it is a *musicale* or night at the theater, I believe I shall do myself proudly." She bit her lip and gave him a saucy grin.

"I cannot wait for you to watch your first theater performance. I assure you, there is nothing I would be more eager to see than your entertainment of the stage."

"Are you implying that you would go to the theater simply to watch me watch the stage?"

"Of course."

Shaking her head, she impishly replied, "You, my dear, *are* a simpleton."

"Do you intend to call me names and mock my intelligence the whole time we are acquainted with each other?"

"Most probably, yes. I cannot help myself—it slips out so easily when you are near."

He wrapped his arms around her and caught her up. "Ha! I knew you were a minx the moment I set eyes upon you."

Jenni James

"The moment you set eyes upon me, you were asking me to dance, so I must not have been that much of a minx in your eyes. Alas, it was an invitation I turned down for reasons you understand much better now."

They heard giggling nearby. Compton released her at once, and safely tucked her hand into his elbow again. "No, you are wrong. The very first time I saw you was last year, when you were racing up the steps of your brother's home with your poor maid several meters away attempting to keep up."

"You never said."

"'Tis true. I was with Lord Hamson and inquired immediately who you were, as I had not seen such an attractive gel anywhere else during the Season."

"Let me guess. He was quick to inform you I was Lady Ice and a bluestocking, no doubt, who deserved no attentions from any man."

"On the contrary. He expressed how ardently he admired your beauty and fortune, and how several men would be more than willing to snatch you up—if you would ever give any of them an opportunity to do so."

"Oh, bosh! He said nothing of the sort, so do not attempt to bewilder me. I am not a green girl, you know. Now out with the true, and not another outrageous bouncer!"

Compton laughed, and grew even fonder of the lady than before. "Very well, he said he believed you were Lord Melbourne's half-sister, and knew nothing else besides that."

"Now, that is an account I can trust." She sighed. "Though why you insist on filling my head with this nonsense that many men find me attractive and the like is beyond me."

"You are correct, my fair lady. I should not be so remiss, for if you truly understood your worth, you would be running from me."

Then, before Lacey could argue with him further, the fireworks began to explode into the sky. Their loud bangs and sparkling falling stars captivated Lacey in the most enjoyable ways. He held her hand and took her round the bend toward where everyone was gathering in the park to watch the display. Everyone but him. Her genuine delightful reactions were too incomparable, and he simply could not tear his eyes from watching her artless joy.

"It is the most magical thing I have ever seen," she exclaimed. "Indeed, this must be magic! For what else would cause such exquisiteness and glitter in the sky as this?"

Compton could kick himself for considering her cold and unfeeling, even for a moment! Her complete enthusiasm and elation exuded a warmth unlike any of the *ton*. Thankfully, she had not been tainted by their sharp opinions and false attitudes. No other woman would sit here with such rapt, giddy attention as she expressed now—their faces would be painted with jaded ennui. Nay, she was utterly, wholly present, and perfect in every way.

CHAPER TWENTY-SEVEN:

Lacey danced about in her room later that night, tossing her clothes high into the air and whirling about as she attempted to catch them. Never had she felt so elated with the world. Never had she spent so many days in a row without thinking of life's hardships and her resolve to sort them all.

Locking her door, she skipped to the chaise lounge and threw herself dramatically upon it, her happy face looking to the sky beyond the window and daring to presume she could see the stars aligning for her cheerful future. Finally, she felt there was a future for her, something to embrace and look forward to.

And then for no particular reason at all, she began to weep. So full of emotion was she that her tears came quickly and sharply, unlike anything before. Indeed, there was no warning, as if all this time, she had been holding her soul together—reminding that fragile being day by day that no one would ever remember her or see her again. Not truly. Not enough to wish to be with her and marry her. Lacey had given that delusion up long ago. She had resigned herself to become an old maid, and never envisioned that a gentleman could want her once he knew her.

Lacey's days were spent in busy agitation, filling her heart with so much worry for others that she had not believed anyone could possibly wish to worry for her. Until now. Oh, she was a foolish girl indeed! A happy, horridly foolish girl.

Because she did dream now. She did believe. And even if it all came to naught, oh, how she had lived in this last little while! How she soared! And to think—Lord Compton kissed her!

That man did more for her fragile awareness than she could ever have done for herself. One does not believe one is worth loving if all she knows is that she is not. Lacey curled up in her nightdress, clutching a small round pillow, her shoulders shaking as she released those tears.

Tears of worthlessness, shame, loneliness, self-pity, grief, and now her new optimistic tears of exuberant joy, hope, faith in tomorrow, and tears of love. She sobbed the hardest at those. God must be a caring being to be sure to send such a man as Lord Compton to her.

His past was no longer insufferable, and she had learned the hardest lesson of all—judgement. She had cruelly judged the man she would one day love with all her heart, for she did. Yet first, she had to free herself of all the disdain she had cloaked about her like a shield. It must flee now because she was alive once more.

Finally, fortunately, there was no room for anything in her heart but warmth, happiness, and love.

How she had waited for the time when she could be free. Tomorrow was a new dawn, and with that dawn, a new Lady Lamb, a lady who believed in fate, goodness, and the reality that she was wanted, cared for. Loved.

Lacey stayed that night curled up in the chaise lounge, with the little white pillow tucked into her arms until she fell asleep. Later, when Chull knocked and then unlocked the door for the maid to light the fire, she walked over to the sleeping princess. Lady Lamb was smiling like an angel. The tears still stained her cheeks, but they must have been tears of joy, for no one smiled like that unless they were exceedingly blessed. Chull did not dare disturb her, and so gently placed a knitted blanket upon the sweetheart and tiptoed with the maid out of the room, shutting the door behind them both.

The next morning, the weather was dismal and rain splattered, but Lacey was not gloomy in the least. Her soul felt as though it had been kissed by sunshine, so bright and tall and magnificent was she. There was no wrong she could not right, no demon she could not overcome, and no worry she could not flit away. Lady Lacey Lamb was an incredible force to be reckoned with, and she had much restitution to make.

After luncheon, ignoring the chattering of Pantersby, flying by him with a jovial kiss upon his wary cheek, Lady Lamb climbed into her closed carriage with a very flustered Mrs. Crabtree to brave the wilds of London's spring storms.

Her first stop was at White's, where the shocked Mrs. Crabtree felt it much better for her nerves to stay in the coach than to walk into the gentlemen's club and tarnish her reputation, as Lacey was wont to do. Lady Lamb had one desire, and she had no intention of vacating the premises until it was fulfilled.

Several heads turned as she walked firmly into the darkened, finely upholstered lounge area. Her umbrella was soaking and hanging from her arm, as it was too early for a man to be at the door to take it from her. "Where do I go to remove bets?" she asked the four or five gentlemen who were in the club that morning.

Without saying a word, one of them pointed to the counter behind her, where a finely dressed man about twice her age stood with his mouth agape.

"Are all of you afraid of women, then?" she asked with a stubborn tilt to her lips. "Hello, good sir." She turned fully and addressed the man. "I am Lady Lamb, and I wish to pay the fine and remove the wager my brother, Lord Melbourne, placed on my behalf. It involves Lord Compton and myself."

"My lady, I know who you are."

"Good. Then kindly go about doing as I have asked."

"Yes, my lady, I would instantly. However, I am not sure I can."

She blinked. "Why ever not?"

"Because you are a lady, my lady."

Lacey could feel her pulse quicken in annoyance. She spoke slowly and forcefully. "Yes. I know I am a woman. The bet pertains to me. I asked my brother to place it, and therefore, it is mine. I would like to remove it now. Lord Compton has won. For that reason, please make haste. I have other errands to attend to."

"But he cannot have won, my lady!"

Was her whole day going to be this full of incompetent people? Lacey took a deep breath to calm her irritation. "Is that because I am a lady as well?" she asked, one fine brow rising in disdain.

His hands visibly shook as he glanced around the room for help. No one came to his rescue.

"My lady, Lord Compton cannot win because you already have."

CHAPTER TWENTY-EIGHT:

Lacey could not believe her ears. "I beg your pardon. Pray, can you repeat yourself?"

The man swallowed and pulled three large betting books out from under the counter. Opening one, he dragged his finger down rows of scripted words until he came to hers. "Do you see this?" He turned the book for her to see. "This is Lord Melbourne's bet, made on your behalf." He then pointed to scores of smaller lines and figures to the side of it. "Here is the list of those who wagered in your favor." Then he pointed to a smaller list. "These are those who have bet against you winning. And this," he pointed to the bottom, "is Lord Compton's bet in your favor. He has taken all of his earnings and improperly bet against himself."

The man scrambled and opened a pouch, pulling out a few coins and two notes. "This is essentially a gift for you, my lady. It is from Lord Compton, and is considered a favor for his conceding the wager."

She felt as if her mind was muddled. "Lord Compton has conceded the wager? Are you certain?"

"Very much so, my lady. He was here just yesterday, or the day before, I believe. Here, I will show you." He flipped a few pages backward and found the bet that was now crossed out with the words, "Lord Compton acknowledges Lady Lamb's superiority, and pledges all winnings in her favor."

"Well, what does it mean?"

"It means he has fallen in love with you, and knows it."

Her gloved hand covered her mouth most daintily. Her breathing had become too labored to think, and her ears too muffled to hear. "Forgive me. It would seem I have no reason to be here after all." She attempted to smile as she clutched the umbrella and turned to leave.

"Wait, my lady. You have forgotten your gift."

"Thank you." In a blur, she placed the money in her reticule and dazedly walked out of the club. She all but forgot to bring her umbrella up as she stepped into the London haze, but caught the first of several drops and quickly opened it again.

"Well, that was the most astounding thing I have ever experienced," Lady Lamb said as she climbed into the seat across from Mrs. Crabtree.

"Oh, I am sorry it was so dreadful for you! I warned how it might be, but would you listen? No. You had to go in."

Lacey closed her eyes and sighed. "My dear Mrs. Crabtree, going into White's was not what I was referring to. However, being told I have won the bet I had hoped to abolish was completely shocking, I assure you."

Mrs. Crabtree dropped the lacey handkerchief she had been dramatically holding over her mouth and gasped. "Won the bet? You? Does that mean Lord Compton is—?"

"Yes, apparently he has beat me to it and proclaimed to the world he is in love with me. Though how he managed to keep Lord Hamson and Lord Atten from telling me last evening, I do not know, yet I imagine it must have involved threats."

Mrs. Crabtree's eyes grew huge. "Threats?"

Why did she bring Mrs. Crabtree? What concoction of madness convinced her this particular woman would help lend a distinct respectability?

She tapped the top of her coach with the umbrella. "To Gunter's, please."

"Yes, my lady," her coachman called down just before she felt the carriage lurch into London's traffic and rain. She felt a momentary stab of guilt for making John work in such conditions, but she did offer him the weekend off in exchange, which he was heartily glad for.

As they approached the tea shop on Berkeley Square, she said to Mrs. Crabtree, "We are a bit early for our next appointment, and so we will grab a bite to eat until he comes. Will that appease you for the folly of taking us both out into this weather?"

Lacey could see Mrs. Crabtree perk up considerably at the thought of a lovely tea at Gunter's. "What is England without her rain?" she asked.

"Quite right." As Lacey stepped down from the coach and into the shop, once again she felt as though the world was completely in her favor. There was nothing she could not accomplish today if she attempted it.

After a table had been procured for them and a large pot of Gunter's tea arrived with scones and jams and dainty sandwiches, a much more settled Mrs. Crabtree asked, "Who is the appointment with, my dear?"

"When I awoke this morning, I immediately sent out a letter to meet with a gentleman here at Gunter's."

"Lord Compton?"

"No, but I am hoping it will benefit Lord Compton immensely. He has told me about his interest in government, hence why I sent for Lord Stanthorpe to meet with me. The Speaker of the House has previously promised to help Lord Compton. I am merely reminding him of it."

"Is it wise to meddle?" Mrs. Crabtree asked, taking a sip of tea.

A flash of fear came over Lacey. "Do you believe this is meddling?"

"If I were Lord Compton, I would suddenly feel very pressured indeed if the woman I loved was now forcing me into politics."

"Oh, dear! I had not thought of that." She glanced around the busy place. "I wonder if there is time to send a notice of regret and return home."

"I doubt not, for that is the very man you seek right there. I recognize him from the ball he hosted." Mrs. Crabtree pointed behind Lacey. "And I fear he is heading this way."

CHAPTER TWENTY-NINE:

"Gooday, Lady Lamb, Mrs. Crabtree." Lord Stanthorpe nodded politely to them both. "I have ordered us all ices that will be ready shortly, and was wondering, since this rain has begun to let up, if you would like to walk with me for a moment while we eat. I find that sitting so long in my office can cause my old legs to suffer."

"Yes, but I fear I have brought you on a fool's errand, my lord," Lacey said as she stood up. "I do not wish to be thought of as meddling, as it is the exact opposite I was hoping to achieve, and now I cannot see it in any other light than just that—meddling. Therefore, I beg of you to forgive me, but I do not find it a necessity to speak with you after all."

He waved his hand and gestured for her to seat herself again, then pointed to a chair nearby. "Do you mind if I sit with you until the ices arrive?"

"By all means, please do."

He nodded and sat down and then smiled. "I must say, meddling or not, I found your letter to be very diverting, Lady Lamb, and one I will not forget for some time."

If mortification were an illness one could die from, Lacey might be very close to expiring in her chair. "Oh, do not mention it. I am so ashamed now. And to think I brought the Speaker of the House away from Parliament to a public establishment in the middle of the afternoon."

"Do not be so hard on yourself. Even politicians must eat from time to time. I agreed to meet with you once the first sitting ended and before the second began. I normally would not have agreed to do so, especially at such a bustling place as Gunter's, but seeing as the invitation was from you, I could not resist. And my wife, Lady Stanthorpe, lent her approval when I sent a messenger earlier explaining the situation." He leaned forward. "I suppose this has something to do with young Lord Compton joining Parliament, does it not?"

Lacey gasped, and Mrs. Crabtree nearly dropped her teacup. "However did you know?" Lacey asked him.

Lord Stanthorpe chuckled. "I am so exceptionally glad I came today. This will prove to be the most magnificent thing that happens all year, I am certain of it."

"Lord Stanthorpe, you cannot know the half of it." Lacey's hands shook as she drained her cup of tea. "Where are my manners? Would you like a cup?"

"Perhaps in a moment. Currently, this meeting has been much too entertaining to think of tea."

She had a very strong suspicion that the older man was mocking her, yet in a playful manner. "What is it that you know and I do not?"

"I confess, I am caught between revealing it all to you myself or letting Lord Compton have the honors. Either way, we have had some tremendous luck the last twenty-four hours, and it would seem an opening may become available much sooner than either of us anticipated. Though he will not be able to present until next year, he could begin shadowing and sitting in Parliament as early as a fortnight."

Lacey stared at the lord dumbfounded, not knowing what words to utter next, so overwhelmed was she by this admission. Then slowly, one thing—nay, two things—began to be more prominent than the rest. "Alistair has previously spoken with you?"

Lord Stanthorpe smiled. "Yes."

That must have been the news he was hesitant to share, afraid he might not actually get into government. "And the other? You mentioned something to do with luck?"

"Well, not so fortunate for the two men who passed on, one last night and then this morning, but extremely providential for the young lord and his hoping to occupy one of those seats."

Her face fell. "That is a shame to lose two lords in one year, let alone within twenty-four hours. May I ask who they were?"

"In respect of the families, we are not making it public at this time, but it should be in all the papers by four. Rest assured, each of them had grown ill and had not attended since last year. It was, shall we say, inevitable?"

It was all too much. Lacey had experienced so many rushes of emotion in the last few hours, she felt as though she were being smothered by several blankets at once. Lord Stanthorpe, thankfully, turned his attention to Mrs. Crabtree and her adulations of their ball, allowing Lacey some time to compose herself.

Lacey looked out the window and attempted to sort her thoughts, yet her mind would not be calmed. Her most fervent desire was to see Lord Compton immediately.

"I believe you may need to go home and rest, Lady Lamb. I fear the rain may have fatigued you greater than you realize," Mrs. Crabtree observed once they had settled into an easy silence.

Yes. Leave at once! She turned toward them both. "Perhaps. Forgive me, but I think we shall forgo the ices and take our leave." Lacey stood up and Mrs. Crabtree was quick to follow, as was Lord Stanthorpe as well.

"Do not worry about the ices. I am certain I can find a place for such a delicious dessert." The lord patted his middle and chuckled as the ladies bid him adieu at the door.

"I have never met a more informal man in all my life!" Mrs. Crabtree gasped, scandalized as she flipped open her umbrella and waited for the carriage. "How could he say the rain had let up? It must be twice as hard now than before we entered."

Lacey grinned absentmindedly. Honestly, she had not considered his manners, or the rain. All she knew was that Lord Stanthorpe was remarkably at ease and would no doubt prove to be an abundant friend to them shortly. Perhaps she would not feel so ashamed about waltzing on his dance floor again.

CHAPTER THIRTY:

Later that evening, as the servants announced Lord Compton's visit to Green Street, Lacey's heart began to race over again. She smoothed out her blue-and-white gown and waited for him as he entered the drawing room with a beaming smile on his face.

"Did you truly go to White's to cry off the bet this morning?" Alistair walked right up to her and bussed her on the cheek. "It is all anyone is speaking of this evening."

"Yes, though are you not a little shocked that I did so?"

"Shocked?" He laughed and spun her around. "At something you would do? Never!" Then he slowly lowered her until his lips found hers. When he pulled back, he asked, "And you spoke with Lord Stanthorpe on my behalf at Gunter's as well?"

She bit her lip and looked away as she attempted to hide her flushing face.

"Truly, the rumors have been so great, I could not believe they were actually plausible. I did not learn of Lord

Stanthorpe until I returned home, but my servants were all lively. So I came immediately to ask it of you."

"Yes, it is all true. Unfortunately so."

"So the Speaker of the House came and met you at Gunter's, and you spoke of me?"

"We spoke of how you had already met with him, and I was attempting to achieve something that had previously happened. Honestly, I am so ashamed. Can we not talk of something else?"

"Yes." He kissed her again, and then again. "My sweet, darling, meddling Lady Lamb."

She winced and pulled away. "Oh, do not say that I am meddling."

Alistair chuckled and asked, "Shall we call you inquisitive, then? Is that a better word for it?"

Pushing against him, she turned and covered her face with her hands.

"Very well, you win. I shall behave. Let us talk about this bet instead." He set his hands gently on her shoulders. "I warned Hamson and Atten not to say a word to you at Vauxhall, but I honestly believed you would have heard from someone before now."

"Heard that you had fallen head over heels in love with me?" She turned slightly to look over her shoulder at him.

"Yes, you minx, precisely that."

Lacey giggled and reached back, bringing him round to face her. "I do not know why you have, but I am so unbelievably happy."

"My dear Lacey, I most likely fell in love with you the day your counter bet was placed."

"Then? Are you sure?"

"Yes, but I had not believed myself fully tumbled until we waltzed."

She shook her head. "What a hopeless mess this is! Certainly not your typical romance at all. Wagers and scandalous activity—"

"From the very moment we met!"

"Oh, bosh! You needed me to refuse you the dance. You deserved it, even."

"Yes, I deserved to be given the cut direct by the most beautiful woman in the room. Oh, Lacey, I know I have said it before, but thank you for your excessive patience with me. I will continue to drive you mad and do things I ought not and no doubt blunder about with your feelings more times than not." He held her hands. "But believe me, my dear, no man in all of England has ever felt for a lady as I do you. And it would be an incredibly adventurous journey if you would consent to marry this dastardly, intolerable scoundrel."

"My lord, you are exceedingly dastardly, it is true, and you give the most intolerably heart-melting kisses any woman could ask for, yet it is the scoundrel in you I have fallen most in love with. Because, my dear, without him, you would have never tolerated such a scapegrace and unbearable scamp as me." She wrapped her arms about his tall broad shoulders and grinned into his devastatingly handsome face and whispered, "Yes! I cannot imagine my world happier, or more complete, without you."

"Then I had better ask for your hand directly, for who could deny such an imp as you anything?"

When he did nothing but stare at her, she exclaimed perplexedly, "Alistair, if that is your way of proposing, I suggest you make it up to me immediately so that I may answer you."

Alistair bent down and claimed her mouth in the most ardent of kisses yet. So thorough was that kiss that neither of them heard the giggled whispers of the most excited butler, housekeeper, and cook who have ever lived on Green Street. For their prayers had most definitely been answered—Lady Lamb finally knew what it was like to fall in love.

Pantersby cleared his throat and held out his hand near the door of the drawing room where they had been listening. Grumbling, Cook and Chull reached into their pockets, pulled out two shillings each, and handed them over to the smug butler. "Never bet on a definite wager, dearies. Never do."

THE END

And now for a peek at

Lord Romney's Exquisite Widow

by Jenni James,

CHAPTER ONE:

Lady Catherine Elizabeth Anne Marsham, Dowager Viscountess of the late Earl of Romney, turned from her rather bewildered position of staring out the second-best parlor's full window at Moat House in Kent. She had been blindly gazing at the horridly gray torrent of England's most dismal winter on record. There had not been even a hint of snow to recommend itself this early December day, and with the rain spitting out as it had been wont to do all fall, there looked to be no reprieve from such gloominess in the near future.

She sighed, walked over to the large dark-blue sofa, and picked up her embroidery, a picture of a happy kitten, a Christmas present for her step-grandson Joshua Marsham, the future Earl of Romney. This embroidery had no end in sight, like the continual rain before her. Truly, it felt as though she would never finish the thing.

It was no wonder Catherine was out of sorts. Tomorrow, it would be one year since her husband had passed on and her life had altered once again. She tossed the sewing upon the seat next to her and looked at her black dress. Though it was customary to begin lightening her clothing with purples and grays before now, Catherine had decided to see it through and wear black for the complete mourning period.

Lord Romney, bless his heart, had been deeply in love with his previous wife and their children long before he met Catherine in London three years prior. Indeed, as the older gentleman walked with his cane around the assembly hall with her hand in the crook of his elbow, he had only talked of the graces and marvels of his late wife. So much so that it was a complete and utter shock when he came the week next to offer for Catherine's hand, as well as bringing a generous gift to her parents of some eight thousand pounds to put their affairs to rights. How he had known they were short on money, one could never guess. Her father had been a wise man and gracefully accepted the amount, and Catherine was sold, like cattle, in a very backwards and unlikely union of souls.

She was exceptionally young to have a title, as her mother reminded her daily before she and the old earl wed. And it was her exquisite beauty that captured the heart of the man who promised to keep her well endowed with a small fortune and pin money of her own after he was deceased. He was lonely, and her dear face reminded him of his cherished wife in her younger days. Which is how Catherine found herself at merely nineteen, married to the well-respected Earl of Romney, whose children, ranging from twenty to twenty-eight, were all older than she.

Now at nearly twenty-two, she was a widow of some consequence whose stepson, the new Early of Romney, Charles, and his wife, Sophia, were eager to make Moat House their home. Catherine had been planning for some time what to do, and thought it best to rent some rooms in

Jenni James

Bath for a while before deciding where to purchase a nice house for herself and hide away.

Sophia walked into the room, smiling. "Are you eager for tomorrow? To finally cast off your blacks and be in color again?"

Catherine looked up as the dark-haired beauty approached, picked up Catherine's embroidery hoop, and then sat down next to her. She was dressed in a lovely green gown with darker forest-colored stripes.

"I was only this moment marveling at the change in clothing on the morrow. I have had a few dresses made up, but it will be strange to put them on so soon. Perhaps I should start with darker gowns, like you have, and then work my way back into lighter colors."

Sophia shook her head and laughed. "Only you would be so concerned about propriety. Come now, tell me all about your plans. Are you still set on Bath and then a place somewhere in the country?"

"Do I have another choice?" At three years older, Sophia had become much more a friend or sister than a stepdaughter could ever be.

"Of course there are other choices, Catherine!" She scooted closer in eagerness. "I am bursting with the idea Charles and I came up with last evening before nodding off, and I think you will love the notion as well."

"It has something to do with me, I gather?" They were too kind to her.

Sophia grinned excitedly and grabbed each of Catherine's hands. "We are both in agreement, and believe you should accompany us to London for the Season in January!"

Catherine nearly choked as she abruptly started to have a coughing fit.

"Catherine, do not be like this, dear. You are too young to hide yourself away, and you have never known love before. No, we cannot see you shut up and hidden from the world before you have had a chance to live." Sophia paused. "Say, are you well? Indeed, you are looking rather pale." She turned to the footman. "Fetch the dowager a glass of water, please. And hurry."

"I am fine," Catherine protested. "I was a little taken aback."

"Good. I am glad of it. However, we are perfectly serious in asking you to come with us to London."

"I thought you were meaning to stay in Kent while Charles went for Parliament this year."

"Yes, that was our intention. However, our plans have changed. We wish to open up the house in London to be together, and are ever so eager to see you come with us."

"Sophia, firstly, to alter your plans for me is too much. I know you would rather be here in the country. And secondly, after one marriage, I have no desire to wed again."

"Yes, we know this, but dear, I cannot stress enough— though I loved my dear father-in-law, you were not in a real marriage. It was for suitability only, and I cannot bear to imagine you continuing on thus. You are young. You should rally and come out and enjoy yourself for once."

Catherine imagined what life would be like had she not wed so early. She had not even had a full Season before she had been swept off the marriage mart. Her heart began to beat rather quickly as she recalled two exceptional dances with Lord Hamson before her father accepted Lord Romney's proposals. It was folly indeed to remember the dashing light-haired lord. No doubt he had wed some other fortunate girl years ago. Her hands trembled as she pondered what had become of the first man she had set her cap on.

Yet to bring up his name to Sophia now would be crass and heartless, and Catherine was neither of those things. "I do not know if I have the courage to face them all again." It was best to keep the past in the past.

"Courage?" She smirked. "You have plenty of courage. What you lack is determination."

"No. I am very determined to head to Bath."

"Catherine, please, I beg of you. Come. It is time. You have allowed yourself to be buried away in this house for far too long. Dearest, enough. You have lost your vivacity, and it pains me greatly to see you reduced so. I will not take no for an answer." She looked imploringly at Catherine, and then tapped her lips with one slender finger. "Perhaps you could attempt to enjoy yourself for a fortnight or two. If after one month, you do not wish to remain, we will gladly take you on to Bath. Would that do?"

Catherine grinned and shook her head. "You are incorrigible."

"No, I have finally grown enough to admit the truth." She leaned into the soft back of the sofa. "I was so very skeptical when Charles' papa remarried. I could not imagine that you would become as dear to me as you are now. My thoughts, before meeting you, often turned to moneygrubbing, I am sad to admit. And then you came. And you were kind and gracious, and loved me in spite of my arrogance, and slowly but surely won over everyone around you, including the staff! I still cannot get Cook to make me those cherry tarts she is always presenting you with. And now, here we are, the best of friends. You, wiser and a greater mother than my own, and yet you carry this overbearing sadness."

Catherine let out a sigh of resignation. It did no good to dispute with Sophia. Eventually, she would wear her down, and Catherine would find herself traveling west for the Season despite anything she would have said otherwise. "You flatter me. I do not feel worthy of such attention as this. Truly, it is ridiculous." Could it be possible? Could she be given another chance at finding love? "However, if you wish it of me, you know I cannot deny you—I will come to London for one month. And if life is dismal, I shall be much happier at Bath, where it is a bit quieter, in a community full of things to do that are more to pace with that of a dowager widow."

Jenni James is the busy mother of ten kids and has over twenty-five published book babies. She's an award-winning, best-selling author who works full-time from home and dreams about magical things and then writes about what she dreams. Some of her works include The Jane Austen Diaries (*Pride & Popularity*, *Emmalee*, *Persuaded*...), The Jenni James Faerie Tale Collection (*Cinderella*, *Snow White*, *Rumplestiltskin*, *Beauty and the Beast*...), the Andy & Annie series for children, *Revitalizing Jane: Drowning*, *My Paranormal Life*, *Not Cinderella's Type*, and the Austen in Love Series. When she isn't writing up a storm, she's chasing her kids around their new cottage and farm in Fountain Green, entertaining friends at home, or kissing her amazingly hunky hubby. Her life is full of laughter, crazy, and sunshine.

You can follow her on twitter: @Jenni_James
Facebook: authorjennijames
Instagram: authorjennijames
She loves to hear from her readers. You can contact her via—
Email: thejennijames@gmail.com

Snail Mail:
Jenni James
PO Box 449
Fountain Green, UT 84632

Other books by Jenni James:

The Jane Austen Diaries

Pride & Popularity

Persuaded

Emmalee

Mansfield Ranch

Northanger Alibi

Sensible & Sensational

Regency Romance

The Bluestocking and the Dastardly, Intolerable
Scoundrel

Lord Romney's Exquisite Widow

Lord Atten Meets His Match (2017)

Cinderella and the Phantom Prince

Austen in Love

My Pride, His Prejudice

Jane & Bingley

My Persuasion

Modern Fairy Tales

Not Cinderella's Type

Sleeping Beauty: Back to Reality

Beauty IS the Beast

Children's Book:

Andy & Annie: A Ghost Story

Andy & Annie: Greeny Meany

Prince Tennyson

Women's Fiction

Revitalizing Jane: Drowning

Revitalizing Jane: Swimming (2017)

Revitalizing Jane: Crawling (2017)

Jenni James Faerie Tale Collection

Beauty and the Beast

Sleeping Beauty

Rumplestiltskin

Cinderella

Hansel and Gretel

Jack and the Beanstalk

Snow White

The Frog Prince

The Twelve Dancing Princesses

Rapunzel

The Little Mermaid

Peter Pan

Return to Neverland

Caption Hook

Other Books

Princess and the Pea

My Paranormal Life

CPSIA information can be obtained
at www.ICGtesting.com
Printed in the USA
LVHW05s2340250418
574947LV00007B/131/P

9 781975 823085